THUNDER

A HEROES AND VILLAINS NOVEL

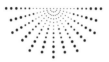

LIZA PENN

NATASHA LUXE

1

DAISY

THE REMOTE TENT IN THE CALIFORNIA DESERT ALREADY has a cult following online. Website after website are devoted to speculation, news, updates, and plans—there's a whole group intending to march on it in two weeks, the idiots; it'll be gone by then. Most of the information on these sites is useless, but this is how I found out which company was behind the funding for the sudden burst of security.

Heroes Org.

Of course it was those fuckers.

I already had plenty of identities locked and loaded for Heroes Org security badges, so it was easy to repurpose one and give *Marcy Lewis* the highest-level clearance possible. Easier still to make the trek to the not-exactly-secret location of the alien ship explosion site.

All that remained after that were a few checkpoints,

some sweet smiles, my distractingly low-cut top, and *bam*—in I go.

The innermost circle of the tent set-up houses the wreckage from the alien ship that mysteriously exploded here a few weeks ago. Rumors abound that it was everything from a crash landing to a domestic airline flight gone wrong. Heroes Org has been fighting to cover it up, of course, just like they cover up *everything*.

But not anymore.

In the wreckage, just like I'd hoped I would, I find a knotted wad of metal that's formed a sort of eggshell around my prize. I double check that it is what I hope it is with a scanner, and when that scanner beeps happily, I grin.

The case I brought will house it securely until I can get it back to my lab—metal-lined with sterlinium plucked from other Heroes Org crash sites.

You'd be amazed what those idiots just leave lying around the California desert. Even when they take security measures like this, it's still laughably easy to just waltz in and pick up what I need.

I'm tempted to give a *thank-you* head nod to the security cameras as I leave, but they'll never be able to piece together these thefts. The disguise I'm wearing couples some face-changing tech—thank you, Anthony Stern and his equally flippant methods of discarding prototypes—and a good ol' fashioned wig.

So even if someone at Heroes Org suspects their

garbage is being rifled through, they'll never know it was me, Daisy Miles, super genius hacker extraordinaire. Which is kind of disappointing, really; I never get any credit for my work.

Yet.

I slip back through the security checkpoints, assuring the guards at each one that the crew coming tomorrow to do the *official removal* will be pleased with their set-up. Flattery never fails to put men at ease. Well, flattery, and huge boobs, both of which I excel in.

The moment I'm back outside the compound, I pull my phone out of my pocket. The door to my jeep unlocks when it senses I'm near, and I dive inside, setting the case gingerly on the seat next to me.

I type out a quick text on my private network.

Package secure. Returning now.

I smile as I hit send. Immediately, a text bubble pops up; I know Ben's been on edge this whole time, despite knowing how good I am at what I do.

Be safe, is his only response.

I hold the phone to my lips, imagining the relief he's feeling—because it's relief I'm feeling too.

Even Heroes Org thinks the explosion destroyed this gem. That's why they've sat on the ruins for so long—they aren't a threat. And sure, it's the Villain Queen Persephone who's finally making a move on clean-up, but even she must think this gem is gone.

All these idiots have no idea what this gem really is. As if something like *this* could be simply *blown up*, even if it was by a so-called *god*.

But no. This gem will outlive us all. It's the reason the destroyer, Niberu, is coming to this planet; it's the reason he'll amass unbeatable power and enslave us all.

But in my hands?

This gem is the reason we'll be able to stop him.

Because Ben and I have a plan.

We have a plan when everyone else on this planet just has fear.

THOR

THUNDER RUMBLES AS I LAND IN THE DESERT. MY hammer slams into the sandy earth, ripples of power cascading around it.

As usual, Thor to the rescue.

I straighten, rolling my shoulders back. My brother Loki is certain he destroyed the power gem, one of the three Niberu hopes to collect in his demonic, demented quest to dominate the universe.

My sister Hela—she goes by the name Persephone in this realm—is convinced my brother failed.

While the two of them bickered about it, I simply left.

I'll find the gem, or its remains, and all will be well. Argument settled.

A massive tent has been tossed over the remains of the shuttle my brother destroyed. I stride up to it.

"Excuse me, sir, you don't have clearance to be

here," says a mere mortal man. He puts up a hand awkwardly, but even he can tell that he cannot stop me if I wish to enter.

"You are here for Heros Org," I say. "Check with the boss."

I smirk at him as he uses one of those ear devices that this realm likes, contacting the "home office." My brother, Loki, is known as Lucas Gardson to these people, the CEO of Heroes Org.

After a moment, the security guard comes back. "I've been told by headquarters that you are allowed entry," he says, but there's something hesitating about the way he speaks.

"Did you communicate with Lucas Gardson directly?" I ask.

The security guard nods, not quite meeting my eyes.

"And what did my brother say in addition to providing me clearance?"

The guard's cheeks flush red. "He, er, he told me to tell you to go fuck yourself, but you're welcome to dig in the rubble if you want, as long as you know you're an insufferable prat who's under his big sister's thumb."

I boom with laughter—ah, that's more like my brother. Loki is ever the mischief-maker. I clap the guard on the back—a bit too hard, judging by the way he staggers. "Good fellow," I tell him, helping him to right himself. "Ah, my brother, such a jokester."

"He, um..." the guard says, trailing behind me as I

kick through the rubble. "Sir, he didn't seem to be joking? He also mentioned that he considers this a betrayal to his honor and that he will personally, um, stab you? Multiple times? He got quite graphic about it."

I laugh again. "Such a kidder," I say. I pause, though. Loki's good-natured pranks do sometimes involve blood. Perhaps I shall have to be a bit wary of my beloved sibling for the next few days. I could speak to his new wife, ask her to distract him from any maiming. Yes. Yes, that's the best plan.

I pause as we enter the main area of destruction. Loki certainly did a number here, using quite a bit of power as he aimed for the gem. Shrapnel and debris are scattered everywhere, huge chunks of metal that aren't even recognizably a part of any ship.

I lift a steel beam and shift it to the side, careful not to toss it in the direction of the mortal who watches me with comically large bug-eyes. "Could you perhaps fetch me some of your Earth coffee?" I ask.

"Earth coffee?" he squeaks.

I nod. "I assumed it was available planet-wide. Black liquid, hot, tastes good?"

"I know what coffee is," the guard says.

"Good, good," I say. "Fetch me some, mortal, please."

Mortal? The guard mouths the words at me, as if he had not heard, although clearly he did, since he repeats it. Still, the good man turns to do my bidding, which I appreciate. Earth coffee is not nearly as good as the drink I had on Asgard—sweetened with wine and nectar, earthy and rich—but it will do.

I survey the wreckage.

I know my brother feels that he destroyed the power gem, and the explosion that happened *was* quite large.

But…

Hela is far wiser. She is the goddess of destruction. And if she says something has not been destroyed, ah, well.

Best to check.

I rummage through the rubble, seeking a shard, a sign, something.

And soon, I see that I was not the first here.

There is a blast radius creeping from the remains of the floor. I piece together twisted metal sheets, flattening them and then fitting them together like a puzzle.

This is where the gem was hit with my brother's magic.

I can see the radius of it, long streaks extending out.

But the epicenter of the blast…it's empty.

"Sir? Your coffee, sir." The security guard presses a paper cup into my hand.

"Mm?" I look down at it confused. My stomach turns. Something's not right. There's all the evidence of where the power gem was, but…if it had been destroyed, surely it would have obliterated far more, caused enough damage to blow up this entire desert, not just the ship. There would not be this starburst-like blast radius in twisted metal.

There would be no evidence left, not if a power gem was destroyed.

I scowl down at the streaks of energy that burned into the metal.

"If you're looking for something specific, maybe that other woman can help you," the security guard says.

"What other woman?" I ask, whirling around to him. While my brother and sister bickered, Loki ensured us both that the area was secure, and no one would breach his security measures.

"She was just here," the security guard continues blithely. "Pretty woman. Took a sample, said the clean-up crew was on their way."

There's *no* fucking way either Loki or Hela would have allowed a human to come to an area where a power gem was. It's one thing to set up guards to ensure no one else would breach the area, but it's impossible either of them allowed a mere mortal access to the site for samples or anything else.

I drop the coffee, tepid brown liquid spilling out. "Who was this mortal who violated my brother's law?" I demand.

The man quails at my look. "We, er—we verified her credentials. It checked out."

I have no time for this foolishness. "Where did she go? What direction?"

The guard looks flustered. "Um—uh—there's only one road. She went south. But she was in a Jeep," he calls as I storm away. "She's been gone more than half an hour! You'll never catch her!"

I snort at that as I fling aside the tent flap.

A mortal may not catch a woman driving in a vehicle.

But I'm a god.

3

DAISY

THE SUN IS SETTING TO MY RIGHT, MY WINDOWS ARE rolled down, radio blaring Beethoven's No. 9, and I have my prize securely on the seat next to me.

So if I drive with my knees for a few miles, playing air violin and really getting into those string swells, can you blame a girl? I'm celebrating, and I've fucking *earned* it.

Once the tent site is far behind me, I rip off my wig and let my long blonde hair stream in the thrashing wind. It's cool for early autumn, and half my mind is already going over the formulas I'll first use with the gem. If we can get it to stabilize Ben's condition so we can control it, then *wham bam thank you ma'am*, Niberu won't know what the fuck hit him when he finally gets around to setting foot on this planet. He thinks he'll find a bunch of defenseless idiot mortals? Well, I mean, he will, but he'll also find *me*. Me and Ben.

God, I feel *good.* When was the last time I felt this good? I want to say with Ben, but he and I both know *that* has been...difficult, lately, to say the least. He tries still, but honestly, there's only so much he can do in his state, and lately I've been too stressed even for that or my own fun. Maybe the gem will change that about him, too.

I bite my lip. It *has* been a while...and this is a mini-celebration, after all.

I slant my chair back a bit and slide my hand down the waistband of the black leggings I'd paired with my low cut shirt for this mission. My boobs are bigger and more impressive, but my ass is pretty memorable too, especially in these leggings, and they give me access now as I delve into my panties and glide my fingers along my mound.

One touch, and my whole body bucks. Thank god I set cruise control. Damn, it really *has* been awhile. Too fucking long.

The orchestra swells again and I go right for my clit. Why wait? I pull back my hood and press my index finger directly on my clit, digging down just to feel the rush of endorphins that scatters across my limbs at the contact.

The desert flies past my Jeep as I keep the wheel centered, but there's no one around for miles, so I don't have to worry about traffic or wandering eyes.

I start rubbing in slow circles, grinding two fingers against my clit, and oh my *god*, why didn't I think to do this when I was so stressed? Ben usually would have encouraged me to, but he's been even more stressed, and with his volatile state, any high emotions are dangerous. God, maybe he needs this as much as I do. When I get back, I'll tell him to fuck his own hand, or I can even get daring and blow him—that'll be a sight.

Now, though, I lean back on the seat, one hand on the wheel, the other rubbing circles on my clit. I break to press three fingers up into my wet pussy, but finding my G-spot at this angle is impossible—I settle for gentle pumps, grinning stupidly at the flurry of pleasure that sends goosebumps down my arms.

Back to my swollen clit, I rub, over and over, building speed. Ben used to do this one thing with his lips—let me see if I can—

I pinch my clit between thumb and forefinger and scrub my fingers together around it.

"Oh fuck," I can't help but gasp. I had no idea I could do that to myself. The orgasm builds, tingles bubbling through my veins, and I keep my clit pinched between my fingers, rubbing it relentlessly from every angle, sensation winding tighter as I force my most sensitive area to come alive, more, more, *more*—

The orgasm hits me and I throw my head back and scream. Pleasure tears up from my pussy and warm waves of it flood out across my body, coming and coming as I keep my clit pinched, milking out every ounce of pleasure I possibly can. My body *needs* this; I've been neglectful of this side of myself for too long—

A violent crash shudders through my car, and it takes me a beat to realize it wasn't just my orgasm; it was actually *my car*.

Something slammed onto the fucking hood.

I blink at the figure fixed to my car, who stares in at me, his eyes ablaze. My hand is still down my pants, but all I can feel now is horror—who the fuck? *What* the fuck?

Oh, shit. Heroes Org sent some lackey after me, didn't they? Fuck, *fuck*—

I slam on my brakes. Whoever it is wasn't expecting that and he goes flying off the hood with a startled bark. It is a *he*, I can see that now for sure, a man in some kind of heavy medieval-looking armor and a red cape, his bright blond hair streaking back as he catches himself on all fours and whips his head up to glare at me through the windshield.

My Jeep skids to a halt, stopping mere inches from his furious face.

I sit there for a long beat. Panting. Heart galloping in my throat. Beethoven's No. 9 petering out to silence on my radio before another piece starts up.

Who the *fuck* is this? I know all the Heroes Org punching bags, and this isn't one.

Which means—*oh fucking hell*.

Is this one of Niberu's?

I rip my hand out of my pants—god, I feel so stupid, masterbating right before *this*—and scramble for my cellphone, but fuck, what can Ben do? He's miles away.

Shit, shit, *shit*.

The medieval armor guy stands up straight. He tosses a hammer into the air and catches it easily, his glare alleviating as he watches me scramble in my Jeep.

"Mortal," his deep voice booms. "Step out of your vehicle slowly, and this will not come to blows."

Will not come to blows? The fuck.

I wrench open my glove compartment and yank out the blaster Ben insisted I carry. I hate weapons—*so* not a warrior—but god am I ever glad he insisted on me carrying one.

The medieval guy takes a heavy step towards my car door. *Shit.* I fumble with the blaster—how the fuck do I work this thing? There, settings of some kind, *1, 2, 3, stun?* The fuck do 1, 2, and 3 do then? God damn you, Ben, why didn't you label this thing better—

The medieval guy gets to my driver's side door. "Mortal. Did you hear me?"

"Fuck OFF!" I swivel, aiming the blaster at the guy even though I have no idea how to use it, but he doesn't need to know that. Jesus Christ, an IQ that can put Anthony Stern to shame, and here I am, outwitted by a *gun*.

The medieval guy gives the blaster an odd look before cocking an eyebrow at me. "Your puny human weapon will not harm me."

Oh fucking hell, he *is* one of Niberu's.

I unfasten my seatbelt and scramble backwards across the center console until I'm sitting on the case containing the gem. "You'll take this gem to Niberu over my dead body."

Medieval guy flinches. "Niberu? I would sooner spit on Asgard's ashes than give that monster anything but a swift and painful death."

That freezes me to the spot. "Then who the fuck do you work for?" I screech.

"None but the salvation of the universe."

My radio is still blaring out classical music, so I'm not sure I heard him right. Who talks like that? I kick the power button to shut off Beethoven—

But medieval guy does *not like that.*

In a flash, he rips the door of my Jeep clean off, his hammer held threateningly in his other hand.

I scream. I scream because I'd *just gotten this Jeep,* and now the door is lying a good twenty yards away, tossed there like a fucking *Frisbee.*

To be fair, he does have the muscles for it, I can see that now. His arms are completely swollen, every tendon and sinew contracted as he holds that hammer up, biceps as big as my head, forearms like tree trunks, all glistening with a fine sheen of sweat, but that's the only sign of exertion anywhere on him.

"OH MY GOD!" I screech and scramble back as far as I can. "What the *hell* is wrong with you?"

"Relinquish the gem, mortal," medieval guy says. "I do not enjoy threatening beautiful women, but I shall if pressed."

4

THOR

I HAD NOT BEEN TELLING FALSEHOODS—THE WOMAN *IS* beautiful. I take a moment to appreciate the luscious curves of her body, the long, blonde hair that shines in the light, the grace she shows even as she musters her courage and her strength, climbing out of her vehicle and cocking her hip at me, one at her waist as she glares. "Why?"

Her demand is befuddling. "Why?" I repeat the question to her.

"Yeah, why?" she says, impatient. "Why should I give the gem to you?"

"Your planet is facing a serious threat that—"

"Yeah, I *know*," she says. "Niberu. Why do you think I stole the gem?"

"I was not aware the humans knew of how deeply dangerous the threat is." Or even *what* the threat is. She

17

had mentioned Niberu, but how can she know the full impact?

She rolls her eyes at me. "Not all of them do, but their ignorance is a result of the sheer and total *incompetence* of Heroes Org. Which means those of us who actually are intelligent enough to see what kind of 'threat' is coming for us have to work twice as hard to get around those buffoons."

I chuckle—oh, my brother would enjoy verbally sparring with this human indeed. For that matter, so do I. But I sober immediately. There is a far graver issue at hand.

"You are not allied with Niberu; you are not allied with Heroes Org, nor the Villain group that often counters them."

"No." She bites the word off at me, as if it were a weapon she'd like to hurtle in my direction.

"Then...for whom do you work?"

She looks at me as if I were truly imbecilic. "I work for—I don't know? Humanity? It's my planet; I have to help save it."

Something swells inside of me. Her passion reminds me of myself, and my own desires to protect my own world. Niberu had originally come to Asgard under the falsehood of negotiations, but he had never intended to work with me or my people. He destroyed my planet, and only a handful of survivors escaped. My siblings are all that remains of my family; my memories are all that remain of my home.

"You have noble ambitions," I tell the maid, for it is truth.

"Yeah? Well, what about *you*, Hercules?"

"I am not this Hercules you speak of. Perhaps our miscommunication has stemmed from your misperception of my identity."

"Do you call ripping the door off my Jeep a *miscommunication?!*" the woman screeches at me. "I know you're not Hercules, my god. What's your name, then?"

"I am Thor, son of Odin."

"You're a Norse *god?*"

I beam at her, pleased with my reputation. "I am a god, and some members of your human society were able to perceive my godhood early on," I say. "Interdimensional time portals let us communicate with early ancestors of your people, who, I confess, did take to worshipping me and some of my compatriots—"

"This is too fucking weird," says the woman who stole a power gem from the wreckage of a space ship in order to fight an alien armada in space. "Next you're going to tell me that Loki's around the corner."

"I do not believe my brother is nearby," I say. "But you did not express a liking for Heroes Org."

"Heroes Org…" she mouths, thinking. "No fucking way! Is Lucas Gardson—oh, Gardson, Asgard, I get it. What the fuck, how did I not realize that before?" She muses, almost forgetting my presence. "Well, I mean, who would have thought ancient fucking *gods* were taking over Heroes Org?"

"I am not ancient, fair maid."

"Fair maid?" the woman glares at me. "My name is Daisy."

A flower on this planet. A weak flower, sometimes seen as a weed. A simple flower that does not match this Valkyrie-like woman with so many thorns.

"I appreciate your quest, Daisy," I say. "But it is futile. Relinquish the gem."

"No," she says.

I blink. "You do not understand the cosmic power with such an item."

"Yes, I do," she says. "And I don't have to prove myself to you. I'm a big girl; I can take care of myself. I have the gem, I'm going to use it, and I'm going to help defeat Niberu. For *my* planet."

There's something about the way she says, "help defeat"—she's not working alone.

And that, more than anything else, makes me...curious.

"Who are you working with?" I ask.

"Not you," Daisy snaps back, "so why do you care?"

"I can help."

She opens her mouth as if to argue more, but then her eyes go past me, to the door of her vehicle that I'd tossed aside.

Then her eyes drift back to me. She holds me in a long, raking gaze, her eyes roving from my helm, to my shoulders, down my navel—lingering there—and further down, my legs, then back up again.

I flex my muscles a little. I mean, just to be sure she sees them.

I am an asset to any team willing to fight Niberu.

"Maybe you can help, Hercules," Daisy says in a tone that lets me know she appreciates my physique.

"My name is Thor," I remind her.

"Yeah, yeah," she says, waving her hand dismissively. "Well, god, are you going to teleport us or something to get us out of the desert? You broke my ride, so, uh…" There it is again, that long, lingering look at me. "Transportation's on you."

5

DAISY

I grab the case containing the gem and hold it tight to my chest. Not that I could do much to stop this guy if he chose to just rip it away from me, but he doesn't make a move to.

Thor—the *actual* Thor; good god, seriously?—scoops me against his chest in one arm. The other he uses to point his hammer ahead of us, and a fucking *portal* opens in the desert landscape.

Of course it does. He landed on my Jeep's roof, didn't he? He had to have popped up from *somewhere*.

Oh my god. What have I done.

I cling to not-Hercules for dear life as he takes a step toward the portal. He gives me an odd look—seems to be a habit of his, like he can't quite figure out my feeble mortal reactions, and I amuse him—and holds me tighter to his chest.

"I will not put you in harm's way, Daisy," he promises, and for some reason, the way he says my name feels way more elegant than anyone's ever said it before. Like he preceded it by *Queen* or *Lady* or some other honorific.

Maybe it's the way he's looking at me. Softness in his eyes, a gentleness that silences my terror.

I believe him.

And I realize, clinging to him, being held by him, that this is the first time in months that I've been touched like this. Cradled and protected, my weight taken by someone else.

My chest squeezes. It isn't Ben's fault. I know that; he knows that; he feels damn horrible about it too. So horrible that he's told me, numerous times, that I should bring someone else into our relationship, someone who can do what he can't anymore.

And being in Thor's arms. His fingers tight around my thigh. The muscles in his shoulder and neck flexing as he twists to stare into my eyes—

This is the first time I've ever really taken Ben's offer seriously.

God, am I just that horny?

"Daisy," Thor rumbles my name.

Yeah, I *am* just that horny, apparently. I hadn't realized how much my body needs this release until in my Jeep. And that was just masterbating—how good would it feel to get absolutely *fucked* again?

Unbidden, I'm hit with an image of this guy

23

throwing me against the side of my Jeep and railing me, hard, in the middle of the desert.

I pinch my eyes shut, knowing my panties are absolutely drenched like I'm some overexcited virgin.

"Yeah?" I manage.

"Where is your lab? I must direct where the portal will take us out."

Here I am daydreaming about letting this massive man have his way with me when there's fucking *work to do*.

And Ben is waiting.

A war of guilt and desire tangles itself in my chest.

I point off southeast. "Five miles that way. Take us that far, and I'll get you the rest of the way."

THOR STEPS us out in what looks like any other part of the desert. His odd mix of interest and confusion has given way to outright distrust—he doesn't believe I've brought him anywhere useful.

To be fair, I'm still doubtful he'll actually offer any sort of viable help, but it's either let him come along, or somehow fight off a literal god. So my hands are kind of tied.

If only, comes another unbidden thought. Fuck me, would my horniness *shut up*?

I scramble out of Thor's arms, not letting myself linger in his warmth and solidity. The case is still tucked against my chest and I stomp across the desert, night's chill starting to permeate the area.

I find the trapdoor easily, and when I enter the code and lift it open, Thor's shock is too satisfying.

"Ah, you humans." He grins, ear to ear. "So ingenious."

"You ain't seen nothing yet, Herc."

"Pardon?"

"It means, *come on*." I dive down the ladder—I've done it enough that I just slide down the rungs and hit the bottom. Thor one-ups me; he *jumps*, landing next to me with a rattling thud that vibrates the metal hallway.

I give him a flat stare as I press a button on the wall. The trapdoor reseals above us.

"You are displeased with me," Thor guesses.

"Displeased with your subtlety," I say. I start walking, and when I hug the case to my chest now, it's suddenly in anxiety. "Just...try to be less cumbersome, all right? My boyfriend's condition is—"

"Boyfriend?"

I look back at Thor. Is that disappointment on his face?

It vanishes. "I should not be surprised that one such as you has already found herself a worthy mate. You fear he will be threatened by me?"

A laugh sticks in my chest. "Absolutely. But not in the way you're thinking."

We get to a door. I turn and press my hand to Thor's chest, stopping him in the center of the hall.

"Just...wait here. Let me explain some things to him before you go charging in all, *Not only do we live in a world with aliens and superheroes, but hey, Norse gods are real, too.*"

Thor's eyes drop to my hand on his chest. I can *feel* his gaze trail up the back of my hand, to my wrist, stroking the side of my arm, the indent of my elbow; and higher, to my shoulder, the dip and rise of my neck.

When finally his eyes reconnect with mine, my mouth is dry, lips parted, every thought completely absent from my brain.

"Of course, Daisy," he says in a low whisper that's far, far too sultry.

Jesus Christ.

I spin away from him, cursing myself, and I hit the security code on the door. It hisses, releasing, and the door swings open.

"Daisy?"

Ben's voice propels me into the room. I make sure to keep the door mostly shut to block Thor's hulking silhouette in the hallway.

The room is exactly how I left it; he's always careful not to move unnecessarily while I'm gone on the chance he hits something that needs immediate repair. But we've designed this room to house him as safe as can be. The ceiling shoots fifty feet over our heads, nearly flush with the surface above, and every wall is lined with steel. There's a massive spread of mattresses and blankets in the far corner that serves as his bed, along with a small kitchen area, a makeshift lab set-up, and electronics Ben can operate either with his voice or using some modified tech.

We've tried to make it as comfortable as possible.

Still. I know what Ben sees in this place.

A cage.

He sits cross legged in the middle of the floor, towering more than twice my height even seated. His eyes brighten at the sight of me and I see his whole body flinch, reaching for me before he rethinks it, his arms staying fisted in his lap.

My heart breaks. My body is still warm from being in Thor's arms.

I hold up the case, smiling through the pain. "Gem acquired."

Ben grins back at me. His smile is the same. His eyes, his features really—everything is just *huge* now. And...purple. His skin is purple. And what muscles he'd had on his once slender frame are exaggerated, shredded and rippling with the effects of the radiation he'd absorbed.

"Any trouble?" Ben's eyes take in the tints of red on my cheeks, my elevated breathing. He can scent things like a hunting dog, a predator's instincts honed to perfection.

I don't even get a chance to say *No* or lie or explain.

27

Ben flies up onto his feet. The whole room quakes.

I stagger, legs planted, one hand flying out. "Ben! Wait! It's fine, really—"

"*WHAT HAPPENED?*" That voice. It isn't *him*. And it's in these moments that the reality of his situation burrows deep into my soul, hearing what we did to him, how very *not himself* he's becoming. There's something monstrous in that voice.

Heroes Org called him the Wreck. For the wreckage he leaves in his wake.

I can see that *thing* in him now. Wild eyes, nostrils flared, something deep and barbarous flaring to life in his body.

"Ben," I say his name as calmly as I can. "It's fine. Nothing happened. But we have a guest."

He holds, his muscles wound, but there is no threat here—not yet, anyway.

So he lowers to one knee.

I walk closer to him. I will *not* fear him, not in this state or any other, and I put my hand on his knee. His skin is rough; the muscles beneath are so flexed it looks painful, the oversized shorts I'd made stretching even with the extra room.

"It's all right," I tell him. "He says he wants to help."

"He?" Ben looks past me, to the cracked door.

"Yeah. He." I sigh, stroking his knee. "Apparently he's a—get this—a Norse god."

Ben's eyebrow arches up and I see the last of the

Wreck settle back into the cage within him. Ben's body doesn't change, though, and that's our problem.

If we could get him to be able to control this whole process—to be *Ben* when he wants to be and *the Wreck* when he chooses—then he'd be unstoppable.

As he is, though, it's too volatile. In this state, he can't control most of what the Wreck chooses to do; and I worry that the parts of him that are *Ben* are slipping more and more each passing day.

"A Norse god," Ben repeats, deadpan.

A really hot Norse god, I think, but I swallow, fighting to keep the flush off my face.

"Yeah. You ready to meet him?"

Ben stares at me for a beat longer. So long that I know he can sense my temperature spiking, can even hear my heart thundering.

I expect him to rage again. It's one thing to offer to bring someone else into our relationship; another entirely for his girlfriend to be standing before him, flushed and clearly aroused by someone else.

And *that isn't even why Thor is here*. Jesus Christ, could my pussy just shut *up* for like *ten minutes*? One orgasm after months without and suddenly all I can think about is sex.

But Ben just smiles.

Like actually smiles.

"Yeah, Daisy," he whispers. "Bring him in."

6

THOR

HE IS MORE BEAST THAN MAN.

And yet there is distinctly something about this monster that still has humanity. Something within him that Daisy clearly loves.

Which makes him worthy in my eyes.

"Greetings," I say, stepping into the room. I'm used to being the biggest being in the vicinity, but this altered human has biceps the size of my waist, feet as wide as my chest.

He's also purple, there's that.

My eyes shift from Ben to Daisy and back again.

"Lab experiment," Ben says. His voice is low, almost grunting.

"It went wrong," Daisy adds.

"I surmised as much," I say.

"It involved radioactive sterlinium," Daisy continues. "We did some tests first, of course, but this was back when Malcolm Odyssey was in charge of Heroes Org, not your brother." She casts a look at Ben. "His brother, the Norse god of trickery, aka Loki, aka Lucas Gardson."

"Well, fuck," the monster says, clearly bemused.

"Right?" Daisy says. Then she turns to me again. "Anyway, Odyssey was big into attempting to make the perfect soldier at the time. And he royally fucked it up all around. Ben was one of the first. He hired our team to biohack a human using a special blend of chemicals, and he rushed the whole thing."

"Hid data," Ben adds.

Daisy nods. "A lot of our tests failed, but he used a different Hero to hack the results, get us to think it was safer. He reasoned that the tests that failed in the lab would work in the field. Anyway, Ben volunteered."

"A super soldier?" I ask.

"Ben has the strength of dozens of men," Daisy says, and although she should be happy about the relative success of the experiment, she's not. She's deeply sad. "He feels no pain, his body regenerates rapidly if he's ever injured, and he can operate at full fighting capacity for a solid week before he needs a rest. They called him the Wreck in Heroes Org."

"I do not understand. How is this not a sign of accomplishment?" I could not match these feats; I am not so diminished as to admit such truths.

Daisy snorts, bitterness wrapped with her sorrow.

31

She grabs a framed picture from a table. "This is Ben before," she says.

There's Daisy, on the arm of a man just a few inches taller than her, with dusty brown hair and hazel eyes and an easy smile. They both wear lab coats.

I look up from the picture into the Wreck's eyes.

Ah. There it is. The eyes still—the eyes are the same.

But every other physical aspect of this man's body is different. Massively muscled, toweringly tall...

They turned a man into a monster.

Suddenly, every other detail of the day hits me. Daisy, getting the gem. Daisy, coming here with it. The power gem, rumored by some to grant wishes.

"No," I say, shaking my head. I look around for the case Daisy carried the gem in. Sensing me, Daisy lunges for it, wrapping her arms around it. "No," I say again, more forcefully.

Ben growls.

Like an animal.

Like a dangerous animal.

A warning, deep and throaty, full of threat. Everyone in the room—including Daisy—freezes.

Ben shakes himself. "You don't tell her what to do," he says, glaring at me. My heart eases a bit. He sounds like a feral beast, but he does still retain his human eyes.

"What do you think you're saying 'no' to?" Daisy asks, more a demand than a question.

"I am...sympathetic to your plight," I say, looking

from Daisy to Ben, nodding, trying to show them my sincerity. "But the gem...it cannot cure him. You associate me with the ancient gods of your planet, but Asgard was lightyears ahead of Earth in terms of technology. I know of radioactive sterlinium—I know...there is no cure."

I expect them to deny it, to protest, to beg me to let them try the power gem. But Daisy merely rolls her eyes. "Yeah," she says as if I am an imbecile. "We know."

"You know?"

"You can't change cells back once they're mutated," Daisy says. "We knew going into this that it would create a permanent change. We'd just trusted Malcolm Odyssey when he told us that Ben would have all the benefits without any of the...negative side effects."

Negative side effects such as growing to a monstrous size and turning purple.

"But then..." I start, most definitely befuddled. "Why do you want the gem? If you know there is no way to use it to cure your paramour, then—"

"My paramour?" Daisy says, laughing.

"Oh, I apologize," I say immediately. "I had thought the two of you were lovers?"

"Oh, we are," Daisy says. "I just haven't heard the word 'paramour' used seriously since I read bad sonnets in English 101."

"Well, we're lovers as best we can be," Ben says. It's more speech from him than he'd said since I entered the room. His eyes—his very human eyes—search mine. "Daisy and I don't believe in marriage or monogamy," he continues. "But yes, we were lovers before. And now...as best I can." He shrugs, the movement powerful enough to upturn a car. "I have to be careful; I never ever want to hurt her. And...the size difference…"

What had once been a man perhaps six feet tall is now a monster easily ten feet tall, broad and musclebound. The implication of what he's saying hits me, and I cringe.

"Why are you telling him so much?" Daisy hisses at Ben.

I look to the man-beast curiously. Why would he reveal so much of his sexual life to me now?

Ben does not look away from me. "All I have ever wanted was to make Daisy happy," he says. "I don't have hang ups about who, exactly, is pleasing her, as long as she is pleased."

My heart kicks up a pace. This is a man who knows true love. This is a man whose selflessness shows a graceful humanity that utterly belies his outward appearance.

My mind whirls as I consider what Ben is saying. He loves Daisy, but their relationship is...open. To be honest, I'm thrilled. That was common in Asgard— people often shared lovers in multiple partnerships, households expanding to include far more than just one couple in a bedroom. Certainly some opted to be exclusive—my brother always preferred to not share his partners with anyone else—but most people on Asgard considered love and love-making to be an open affair involving all willing partners.

My time on Earth has proven, though, that such relationships were not universally approved. It seemed the default of this world was monogamy.

Is that not the case with Ben and Daisy?

I allow myself a moment to visualize it—both Ben and I pleasing Daisy, and Daisy pleasing us in return. I would love to taste her—I could smell her sex on her when I first met her, and it has been driving me mad with lust since then, although I've tried to tamp those desires down. I salivate at the thought. Licking her until she writhes beneath me...filling her with orgasmic ecstasy until she comes apart at my touch...

Daisy, as if guessing my thoughts, has blushed a furious shade of red.

And in her arms, still, is the case with the power gem.

Focus. I have to focus. Perhaps Ben's words were not the invitation I long for, but instead merely a way to distract me so I won't interfere with their plans for the power gem.

"Be that all as it may be," I say, "if you don't intend to attempt a doomed cure for Ben with the gem, then what..."

"I already told you," Daisy says sullenly. "We intend to fight Niberu."

Ben nods, resolute.

Oh—*oh.* I roll back my shoulders, re-examining these humans.

Ben, as the Wreck, is worth an entire army alone.

But with the power gem applied to his considerable strength. Fuck.

It may...it may be enough to take down Niberu.

Without meaning to, I appraise his size again, his skill. "You've trained?"

"For a time," Ben says. "I did work with Heroes Org until it came out how Malcolm betrayed us."

"And how utterly feeble and useless the entire organization is," Daisy adds. "No offense to your brother."

"None taken," I answer, but my mind is still going through the possibilities.

Yes, Niberu has an entire alien armada. But with the head chopped off, if *he* is struck down...they will fall away. The only real threat is Niberu, especially now that his general, Rora, is on our side. He has numbers, but we have a Wreck.

And that may actually be enough.

"Oh, I know that look," Daisy says, excited. "You're weighing our odds and thinking we're right, aren't you?"

I nod slowly, eyes still on Ben. A power gem applied to a mere human's strength would not be enough. It would, actually, likely kill the human. Even I, stronger than most, would be wary of actually applying the gem's powers to my own body. I could see myself trying to fit it to a weapon, my hammer perchance, but…

Radioactive sterlinium in a human host, enhanced by the power gem…

This man may be the greatest weapon the universe has ever seen.

I stare at the pair of them a beat too long. They have a bond I recognize, and Ben's words from before flit through my mind. Are they a pair that are truly open, or was that actually a ruse to distract me? For that matter, do they truly intend to use the gem and power up Ben as the Wreck so that he can defeat Niberu or is *that* a trick?

They seem sincere. They seem…welcoming.

And the truth is, if I could choose, I would want to be united with them. Not just against Niberu, but…more than that. I long for the types of relationships I had on Asgard, for the home I found in others' arms.

I cover my face with my hand, turning away. Perhaps it is the power gem's influence, corrupting my thoughts. I am no longer sure of anything.

7

DAISY

I show Thor to an extra bedroom space—it isn't much, but it has a cot, a private bathroom, a kitchen with some food. In truth, I don't want to give him any reason to run off and spill our locations and secrets to his brother. He seems content enough to help us, but...

"I'm going to get a few things booted up," I tell him as I back out of the room. "I'll let you know when your help is needed."

Thor surveys the small room. If he's disappointed, he doesn't show it.

He faces me again and smiles. "Thank you, Daisy."

My cheeks heat. God save me from the way he says my name. It's innocent yet pleading all at once.

Thor tips his head. "Have I done something wrong again?"

"What?" I look up, brows shooting high. "God, no. Not at all. You're—" *Perfect*, I almost say.

Because a literal god of a man came plummeting out of the sky, and he's hot and courteous and supportive and *hot* and—

"Just rest up. I'll be back," I say, and then I leave, because my horniness is starting to swell over me, and I'm worried I'll drop my panties right there.

I get back to Ben's room and can't bring myself to look at him. I go straight to my lab table and start flipping on machines—I'd built a few prototypes while we were tracking the gems, a bracelet, a chestplate, a helmet, all things I could set the gem in for Ben to wear and hopefully be able to channel its power into his body. It'll take awhile for each of them to boot up, and then for the computer to run simulations with the gem inserted, but I pretend to stay busy, flipping through the last test's readouts.

Ben shifts behind me. "Daisy."

"Hm?" I don't turn.

"What's wrong?"

Fuck him and his perception. Really, he was bad enough being able to sense my moods *before* he got these powers; now? He's insufferable.

I close my eyes and take a deep breath. I don't want to talk about where my thoughts have gone since Thor's arrival. I don't want to talk about my roiling fears now that we have this gem—will it work? Will it make Ben worse? I can guess about results, but it's an *alien gem*. I have no fucking clue what it will do. I just know it's incredibly powerful, and right now, Ben needs something incredibly powerful.

I don't want to talk about any of that.

An idea pulses into my mind.

I put down the papers and turn to face Ben. He tips his head, one knee propped up, elbow resting across it. He looks concerned, and I honestly can't remember the last time he *didn't* look concerned. Or angry. Or scared.

That changes now.

"You know," I bite my lip, "I did something in my Jeep after I got the jewel. And I thought about you while I was doing it."

Christ, how long has it been since we bantered in a sexy way? Long enough that Ben stares at me for a full minute, his eyebrows pinched in utter confusion.

Then it hits him.

He blinks at me. His eyes dip down my body, and he swallows, the force of it bobbing his massive neck. I see his jaw clench, one hand curl into a fist.

"Daisy—"

I lurch forward. "I had no idea how much I needed it, Ben. And I think you do, too."

His eyes find mine again. There's that look of fear. "It's a lot of emotion. The risks—"

"Fuck the risks," I tell him. "I'm tired of thinking about risks. And I know you are, too. So let's just...stop. For once. We'll go slow, okay? Actually—" I grin up at him. "You don't have to do a damn thing if you don't want to. Just watch."

Ben's eyes widen. A smile pulls at the corner of his lips and he runs a hand down his face, scratching his stubble, that smile growing until it's all teeth and desire.

He surveys me again, head to toe.

"All right, then." His voice is a low grumble. "Take your clothes off, Daisy."

I give a giddy squeal. This is the closest we've gotten to sex in *months*, maybe longer, and I feel a surge of wetness between my legs, the telltale tingle of need already rampant and hungry.

I'm still wearing the labcoat, tank top, and leggings from my disguise. I let the coat drop to the floor behind me, but Ben's focus stays on me, just on me, as I reach for the hem of my shirt.

It comes up. Off. I'm not wearing a bra and my breasts spill free, heaving and flushed, my soft pink nipples hardening to points the longer I stand there, topless.

I peek up at Ben. His smile is gone. His eyes are all pupil, and I go rigid, waiting for a growl, a snarl, for some sign that it's the Wreck now, not Ben.

But he nods once, terse. "Keep going."

My hands go to the waistband of my leggings. I move slower now, a thin sliver of fear twisting around my desire—

My pussy clenches, and I feel squelching wetness soak my panties.

Is this turning me on even more? The threat, the toeing the line, the danger?

It's turning Ben on. I can see his massive erection through his shorts, his cock bulging.

We never tried to see if it'd still fit. We just *assumed*, played it safe, because we were so worried about him losing control.

And he could. At any moment.

But *fuck* if that isn't hot as hell.

I slide my leggings off and kick off my shoes too. By the time I'm standing naked in front of Ben, he has his cock out now, fisted in one meaty handy.

He gives it a slow pump. "Finger yourself," he tells me, and I find I *love* this version of Ben, commanding, authoritative. My whole body shudders at the force in his words.

But I shake my head and take a step closer to him. "Give me your hand."

He hesitates, cock still in his palm, before he shifts to lower his free hand to me. I take it between both of mine—laid flat on my chest, it would cover my torso—and peel out his index finger straight.

Then I straddle it.

Ben hisses a breath. "Daisy—"

I start rubbing on him, using his hand as my dildo. His skin is warm and at the first contact of my wet pussy, his finger contracts, arching up, the tip sliding into my cunt.

I gasp, head dipping back, eyes rolling shut. I need

him inside of me. I need *something* inside of me.

My hips rock, clit rubbing on his palm as I push his finger up inside of me. Then another, until he's finger fucking me, just like he used to, only these fingers are *far* larger than anything I've had in me before. The sensation is pain and pleasure mingled just like fear and desire, and it drives effervescence through my limbs, an orgasm building fast and furious and roiling.

"How does it feel?" Ben demands. He sounds livid. A manic kind of livid, and when I look up at him, his face is contorted, suppressing a shout, suppressing the Wreck maybe. His fisted hand jerks his cock in quick, rapid strokes, redness creeping across his purple skin.

"Ben," I pant his name. "It feels so good, baby."

I don't have to move his hand now—I let go, and he finger fucks me himself, pumping his fingers in and out at lightning speed. He bends his thumb down and brushes it across my clit, setting a pace of thrusting in and rubbing that dredges a whimper from the pit of my stomach.

My hands climb up my own body and grab my breasts, squeezing them together, and a growl vibrates in Ben's throat.

"Pinch them," he tells me. "Finger your nipples. Now."

I obey. I take each nipple and pinch the pebbled flesh between my fingers, rolling gently, my eyes on his the whole time.

He winces, a ripple shuddering through him, and

then snaps his eyes shut. "Fuck, Daisy—"

He comes as I do, the orgasms taking us in simultaneous waves of ecstacy. I scream, body convulsing, but Ben drives his fingers deep, holding me up as the walls of my pussy clench greedily around him. I'd thought the orgasm in my Jeep was good? This one rips into me, the kind of orgasm that's almost unsatisfying in that it just makes me immediately want more.

Great arcs of cum shoot between Ben's fingers, sticky white liquid pooling down his legs. He shudders and gasps, bending over to ride the high, a high he hasn't had in far too long.

As I come down, I start to remove his fingers from my pussy, but he stops, holding deep inside of me.

I look up at him, panting, sweat glistening on my skin and his.

Ben's eyes are hard, in pain almost, but he smiles at me. "It's been too long. I never should have—"

"Stop. We both know why we've been cautious. I don't need you to—"

"No." He pushes his fingers deeper and I suck in a breath. "I shouldn't have waited around for you to do this. You've done so much already. I should've taken care of you. And I promise, from now on, I'll take care of this for you."

It's damn near impossible to really hear him when his fingers are gently pulsing inside of me, but I nod, breathless. "Yes. Yes, okay. I can handle that."

"Good. Because that wasn't a question."

8

THOR

WHEN A LADY SCREAMS, IT IS MY OBLIGATION AS A prince of Asgard to check upon her.

But when I open the door and see that the lady in question is screaming in ecstasy while in throes of being thoroughly finger-fucked...

A prince of Asgard would look away.

But fuck, I can't.

I watch as Ben brings Daisy fully to orgasm, his fingers driven all the way inside of her. She tosses her head back, her fingers twisting her own nipples in a way that has me utterly hard.

I shouldn't watch.

I shouldn't watch.

But I can't look away.

My hand goes to my cock, sliding under my waistband. Before I can get off, they finish. I pump hard, but—

45

It's not enough.

They speak in low voices, and I turn away. It was wrong of me to watch, to touch myself…

And then I hear a groan.

Daisy tosses her head back, hair streaming, as she looks over her shoulder. Did she—

Did she see me?

Daisy stands up, legs spread apart, in front of Ben, who's sitting. She leans over, her hands upon his thighs, her ass up in the air, her pussy on full display.

As if she wants me to watch.

No—she can't know I'm here. Staring. Lusting.

I fist my cock again, running my fingers over my shaft, imagining sliding it into Daisy's pussy, thrusting hard and fully into her. The image is so vivid I have to bite back my own groan. Slick fluid drips from my cock, adding to the imagery.

Daisy bends down over Ben's lap. His enormous penis is far too large for her to take into her mouth, but she licks it eagerly, her whole body moving as she works her tongue up and down his cock.

I thrust into my hand, hard, mesmerized by her, the way her body moves, the curves down her back. Her hair splays over his lap, her bare skin milky white and smooth, her breasts swinging freely as she languidly licks all the way up from his balls to the tip of his cock.

Even from here, I can see the way her pink tongue darts out, licking his head, lapping at it like she can't get enough of the taste of him.

I do groan then—I can't help it, it's just too hot.

Ben's hooded eyes glance up. I duck behind the wall, trying to hide, and when I dare to peek out again, his head is tossed back, his gaze away from the door.

But there's a smirk on his face, his lips curving in a knowing way. He did see me. I know he did. But he does nothing but lean against the way, his hips angling further up for Daisy to lick at him.

My balls contract with desire—with *need*—as Daisy mounts one of Ben's broads legs, her bare pussy rubbing against his thigh, grinding down as her back arches, her neck bending to slide her tongue all along his cock.

I can smell it.

That's what drives me wild.

I can *smell* her sex, her body. Even if I were blindfolded, even if I couldn't hear the wet noises of her tongue against his cock, of her pussy sliding along his leg—even if every other sense was blocked, I could walk into this room and *smell* the sex.

It's intoxicating.

That thought makes me hunch over, makes my whole body buck into my hand, thrusting hard.

And then Daisy makes a little noise, a humming sound in the back of her throat. My eyes fly to her. She has both knees on Ben's thigh, her legs spread, her finger lightly playing with herself as she purrs and licks all along his cock. Ben grunts, loud, and it's clear he's close, and fuck, so am I—is he loud enough to cover the sound of my hand, wet and hard, running over my cock? Is her body so focused on him that she won't notice me?

I don't know—and that fear and panic at being caught, of them looking up at me as I jack off to them —it makes me cum so violently that my whole body shakes, hot sperm shooting off and landing with a splatter on the floor as I clutch the doorframe just to keep from falling over.

At the same time, Ben releases, his roar of satisfaction enough to rumble the floor. His fists clench, and the steel bench beneath him crumples to show the outline of his fingers.

Daisy leans back, avoiding the shower of Ben's cum as it explodes from him. I'm still weak from the orgasm watching them gave me, still limply leaning against the door frame as Daisy arches back, tossing her hair behind her. Her breasts thrust out, her long back curves enticingly as she perches on Ben's leg.

Out of the corner of her eye, I think she sees me.

I'm too weak to move.

Her hair falls over her face, but it doesn't hide the smile of satisfaction as she licks her lips.

9

DAISY

I SLEEP BETTER THAN I HAVE IN MONTHS.

The next morning has me humming around the little kitchen in Ben's room, setting coffee to brew, heating a skillet for eggs. Ben watches me from the center of the room, legs folded, but there's a glimmer in his eyes now, an amused sort of joy that looks like he's mulling something over.

"What?" I add a splash of oatmilk to my coffee.

Ben pauses. Then shakes his head. "Nothing." His eyes go to the door. "The god of thunder is back."

There's a knock.

I cock an eyebrow at Ben. He knew Thor was watching us last night too. If *I* realized it, then Ben definitely did, but I didn't say anything purely because *Ben* didn't say anything. But *why* didn't he say anything? He couldn't have been *okay* with it? But he's been saying he's fine with me sleeping with someone

49

else for months...and thinking all of this suddenly makes me feel like I'm caught in a high school love triangle.

A blush climbs my cheeks. Ben's soft smile falls.

"Daisy," he says, "are you all right?"

There's a stark contrast between the way Ben says my name and the way Thor says it. Ben is all deep and vibrating, like the name is caught in his chest, slamming its fist on his throat to break free; Thor says it all light and swift, like the name is sweeping out of him as he drops into a bow.

Both do deeply delicious things to my body.

I shiver and hold my mug between both hands. "I'm fine. Thor, it's open!"

The door swings wide, revealing the god of thunder in all his glory. He isn't wearing quite the same regalia as yesterday, opting for only the airy scarlet tunic that was under his armor and sandals, his hammer hooked around one wrist. His blond hair is pulled back into a knot behind his head.

He looks relaxed too. Like he also slept well.

Gee, I wonder why.

I grin at him over my mug. There's a long moment of silence between him, Ben, and I, and I see red start inching up Thor's face the longer we stand here, not speaking.

"Ah." He clears his throat and awkwardly sets his hammer against the wall. It falls over. He resets it and clears his throat again. "What's on the schedule today?"

And just like that, reality goes crashing through this small moment of enjoyment.

My smile falls. I actually *feel* my happiness freeze and drop like a heavy, dead brick in my stomach.

When my eyes go to Ben now, it's in analysis. We'll need to start testing the gem in the braces I made.

I have no idea what they'll do to him.

It could kill him. Or worse.

I take a swig of coffee and turn to dump the finished eggs on my plate. "First—I need to finish running some tests."

It's a lie.

The tests finished during the night. All readings came back positive, or as positive as I can make out with so very many variables up in the air.

I grab my breakfast and rush between Thor and Ben, who eye each other, communicating something wordlessly. They've barely known each other for a *day* —how is that even possible? But Thor nods at Ben and follows me to the lab space I set up in the corner.

"Daisy," he says. God save me from that *voice*. "How may I help?"

I almost snap at him. How the *fuck* does he *think* he can help?

But he *is* only here to help.

And he's one of the only beings on this planet who has faced Niberu. And walked away.

I start switching on machines, booting up my computer. Absently, I flick on a news channel—

weather report right now—and let it play in the background just for noise, something to cancel out the building cacophony of panic rising up in my brain.

"What's he like?" I ask. "Niberu."

I feel Thor tense. When I turn to face him, sure enough, his hands are in fists, his eyes fixed on the floor between us. Beyond him, Ben watches us, his brow furrowed.

"A scourge," Thor says. His eyes flash up to mine, and for a beat, I see the true god of thunder, someone crackling with lightning, someone deadly. "A ruthless warrior built without mercy or hesitation. He will not be stopped—he believes in the absolute righteousness of his cause."

"Which is?" I drop to sit on a lab chair, coffee forgotten, breakfast going cold.

Thor studies me, his eyebrows pulsing once. "You don't know?"

My eyes go to Ben once before skating back to Thor. "We know he's seeking our destruction. But we don't know much about *why*. Or *how*. Aside from—" I swivel in the chair and click a few buttons on my laptop. The screen goes black, then flashes, centering, clearing—

Dotted across a view of space are hundreds, maybe thousands, of ships.

Niberu's approaching armada.

Thor leans over me. His nearness rushes up on me, stealing my breath in a huff of his scent—the spicy soap

I stocked in the bathroom, but something deeper, pure man musk that has me folding my legs together, suppressing a whimper.

Fuck me, he smells amazing.

I fight not to bend closer to him. His hand rests on my chair's back and he narrows his eyes at the computer screen.

"I have seen images such as this before. A satellite, correct?"

I bob my head.

Focus on the computer screen, Daisy. Not on the way his bicep flexes as he leans his weight forward.

"I hacked Heroes Org's satellite. But in the last few days, the armada has moved close enough to Earth that even low-level telescopes can spot it."

On cue, the news I have playing switches to a segment where crowds are protesting in the streets. The reporter talks about how unrest is growing in response to the recent destruction of the Golden Gate bridge — by someone who was very clearly an alien — and the subsequent ship explosion and Heroes Org's clear attempts at covering it up. Signs say things like *The Truth Is Out There* and *Who Is Protecting Us?*

My eyes linger on that last sign.

Who Is Protecting Us?

Exactly. *Exactly.*

"He wants control."

I turn back to Thor. He doesn't pull away, leaning next to me, his eyes shifting through mine.

"Control?" I ask.

Thor nods. "He, too, has a brace for the power gems. One brace, for all three." He motions to the prototypes I have, the bracelet, the chest piece. "It is called the Crown of Arathustra. The three power gems, when planted in it, will allow Niberu full mind control of every living being in existence."

My body goes immobile. Even Ben goes so still he blurs into the background.

"What?" The question rushes out of me.

Thor nods again, his face solemn, sad, and I know he's seeing something we can't, some memory from long ago. "He will do anything—*anything*—to reclaim those gems. And once he does—"

"He's undefeatable." I look up at Ben. His jaw clenches and he holds my gaze, and I see in him the same swell I'm feeling.

I stand, kicking my chair back. "Then we'll just have to kill him before he gets a hand on the two remaining gems."

The chest plate is the prototype I have the most hope in, mainly because it will fit snugly to Ben's body and be less likely to fly off. It's still not the strongest as far as metal goes, though, but if I can reinforce it with some other pieces I've scavenged, then maybe—

I feel eyes on the side of my head and turn to see both Thor and Ben watching me, simultaneous looks on their faces. Wonder mixed with awe mixed with pride.

I snort. "Well don't just stand there, boys—Mama's got work to do, so make yourselves scarce. I'll let you know when I need you."

Thor picks up my uneaten plate of eggs. "First, you must eat. It will do you no good to work on any empty stomach."

"Thor's right," Ben adds. "If you're going to help me murder the strongest creature in existence, you need food."

I roll my eyes. "God, now I have two of you to baby me?"

"Not *baby*." Thor forks a piece of egg. "Care for. Eat."

He holds the fork up to me.

I give him a sardonic look. He smiles, pushing the fork closer to my lips.

Honestly, I could get used to this.

HER DELICATE LIPS PART AND SHE ACCEPTS THE MORSEL of food I offer her. My cock stirs at the sight, and internally, I curse it. This is not my place.

Focus on the task at hand.

I feel eyes on me, and I glance behind me to see Ben watching the two of us. His jovial friendliess belies the sheer size of him, monstrously huge. His eyes are kind, like he's just casually observing us, but there's worry in my heart at what my mind tells me is forbidden.

Daisy snatches the fork out of my hand. "There's work to do," she reminds me, stuffing the eggs into her mouth and then dropping the fork and bowl in the sink before returning to her lab.

Right. I get up and follow her.

"Tell me about this Crown of Arthrastra," Daisy says, pulling forward a rather impressive looking electromechanical universal testing machine and analyzing the tensile strength of some homebrewed metal alloys.

"Crown of Arathustra," I correct her. "It has a fascinating history, actually—"

"I don't care about the history." Daisy glances up, an apology already painted on her eyes. "I mean, I'm sorry —I'm sure it's fascinating and I don't mean to be rude, it's just…"

"No time for a history lesson," I, the god of thunder, worshipped by the ancient people of her homeworld thanks to a twist in time travel during early portal systems and a comparatively long lifespan, says.

"Sorry?" Daisy cringes.

"It is fine, Daisy," I say, but despite that, her cheeks blush bright red. "The Crown of Arathustra is accented with gold decoration, but the main core of it is silver in appearance, but that is not the metal used."

"Can you tell me about the metal?" Daisy says. "That's actually my biggest concern at the moment. The power gem doesn't interact in the same way as most minerals, and setting it in the right metal is going to be key to get it activating on Ben's body. And then, of course, we need to make sure it's not just secure, but that Ben's form as the Wreck *cannot* destroy it. He tends to go a little—"

"Beserk?" I say, remembering seeing some videos of the Wreck in action that my brother showed me when he took over Heroes Org.

Daisy's brows crinkle. "That's…rude," she says. "He

can't help the way the transformation affected his body—"

"Peace, Daisy," I say, holding up my hand. "I meant like the ancient word 'ber-serk,' a person whose body is taken over by war, who acts methodically, entranced by the fury of battle. There are Old Norse legends of such men."

Daisy frowns, thinking, clearly wondering if perhaps those old legends were linked to what had happened to Ben. I answer her unasked questions. "I met a berserker once. His well had been tainted with sterlinium without his knowledge."

Daisy nods, understanding, then almost visibly shifts that thought back to the crown. "So this silver metal that's not silver. Do you know what it is? An alloy, perhaps?"

"I am unsure," I say. "My sister tested it, but did not have much time before we had to flee. She determined that it was extraordinarily dense. Osmium or iridium, I believe."

"Of course," Daisy groans. "Two rare earth metals, the most expensive and hardest to find."

She turns back to her work, muttering, and I step away, leaving her to her task. I bump into Ben, forgetting his sheer size and miscalculating my steps away.

"She gets so focused in her work," he says, his voice rumbling like thunder.

I nod, both agreeing with Ben and appreciating Daisy.

"I saw you." Ben's voice still holds that deep thunder, but there's a little laughter in it. Meanwhile, my stomach turns, shame rising in me.

"Saw me?" I ask, begging all the gods that perhaps he means something else, not me pleasuring myself to Daisy and Ben's fucking.

"Saw you," he repeats, winking.

"I—I should apologize—"

"You shouldn't," Ben says. "We did not ask you to leave."

"You both knew I…er…watched?" That burning, twisting feeling in my stomach is shame, yes, but also… something else. His acceptance makes me recognize it.

Desire.

"Of course we did," Ben says. His voice is low and rumbling—meant only for me—but I see the way Daisy stiffens at her work table. She's listening.

"You know, you could…" Ben starts.

I raise my hands to make him pause. "My brother is more fluid in his desires, but I prefer only women. I do appreciate the offer," I start.

Ben shakes his head. "I not only prefer only women; I prefer only Daisy," he says. "But I am not selfish in that preference. To me, it feels only natural that everyone would only prefer Daisy." He smiles ruefully.

I glance back over at the worktable. Daisy is furiously working, but I cannot help but feel as if it is a ruse.

"I meant that there are some things I can no longer

do. But I wouldn't mind seeing them be done." Ben gives me a significant look.

Oh. *Oh.* I had watched them; I do not think at all that I would mind if Ben watched me in return. Actually, the idea…

I'm hard, aching. My simple, loose clothing does little to hide the desire rising within me.

Ben glances down, smirking. "Besides, some people work best under stress. I used to be that way. Give me a deadline and I can solve any problem. But Daisy is the opposite. She gets her best ideas when she's *utterly* relaxed. That's been part of the problem, I think. Ever since we realized that I could never go back to the way I was, that I would forever be in the Wreck's body and not my own—she's been stressed. She's given herself deadlines and challenges, and now with Niberu and his armada…"

I almost laugh at that. Niberu's presence is nothing if not stressful.

"She needs to relax," Ben says. "I know my Daisy well enough to know that. And I also know the best way to get her to relax."

I make a noise in the back of my throat, the only sound I feel capable of making. Coherent thought—much less vocalizing it—has long since left me.

"Oh, *fine!*" Daisy says, standing up, her chair making a screeching noise on the floor. "If you two are going to talk about me, you may as well let me in on the conversation!"

Ben laughs, and I get the immediate impression that this is not something unexpected to Daisy. "I just happen to know, my love, that you won the Pulitzer based on work you had after a series of mind-blowing orgasms provided by yours truly," he says. "And this is a little more stressful than that situation. Perhaps double the orgasms would help?"

"I mean, I'm not ever going to say no to that offer," Daisy allows. "Even if Niberu was outside the lab, knocking to get in, I'm getting off first."

"Priorities, my love," Ben says, that deep chuckle weaving through his voice.

Daisy spins around to me. "Look, Ben and I have been discussing an open relationship for a long time, even before his accident transformed his body. We're both pretty comfortable with that. What about you?" She casts an appraising eye at me. Whereas Ben presented the topic with a bit of hesitation, easing me into the idea, Daisy is more blunt, more upfront.

"You've got this old-school Norse medieval thing going for you," Daisy adds, waving her hand to indicate all of me. She turns to Ben. "Did you not even think that maybe he's not into the idea of sharing?"

"My lady," I say, speaking for myself. "I live to serve." I give her a little half-bow which I feel is understated, but which she laughs at.

"You live to serve, huh?" she says. She bends her back, thrusting her breasts out, but it was more a motion meant for her to stretch, ease her muscles, already tight from concentration on working with metals and considering the Crown and the power gems. She cracks her neck, and when she looks up at me, there is a feral look in her eyes, hungry and eager. "Well, if an orgasm is going to help me figure out this whole problem, let's get to it," she says.

"No pressure," Ben adds.

11

DAISY

In theory, this is exactly what I want and need.

In practice, everything feels hopelessly awkward as Thor stands there, staring at me, and Ben watches us both. My hands clench and unclench at my sides and I just think—this is ridiculous, right? I was one of the top scientists at Heroes Org before they went crazy and I left. I don't need... *sex*... to bring my A-game. This will just over complicate an already *way* too complicated situation, and all for what? Because I'm *horny*?

No. Nope. Not happening. Not gonna—

"She's thinking too much," Ben says, his eyes on me, but his words clearly directed at Thor.

A slow grin spreads across Thor's face and he studies me intently. "Ah, I can see her worrying. How should I stop it?"

"Kiss her," Ben says, only it isn't calm, it's a *command*, one I feel jolt straight to my pussy.

Thor takes a step closer to me. Another. I don't move, hands in fists at my sides, eyes unblinking as I watch Thor close the space between us until his body is flush with mine. He's taller than me by nearly a foot, but I don't look up at his face; I keep staring over his shoulder, my breathing escalating with each passing second.

A low grumble vibrates through his chest. "Are you nervous, Daisy? That seems unlike you."

"How do you know?" I pant the question. He doesn't know anything about me. It's been, what, two days since we met?

But the way he brushes the hair over my shoulder, a tender gentleness that sends goosebumps down my arm, is laced with respect and awe.

"I know," Thor whispers. "And what I don't know, I'll learn."

His hand rises to cup my chin, and he lifts my face. I can't help it; my eyes snap to his, and a tremble of anxiety flutters through me.

I'm so aware of his nearness, of the heat coming off his body, of his fingers on my face.

I'm so aware of Ben, next to us, watching, his hard cock straining against his pants.

"Kiss him, Daisy," Ben tells me, a gentle prodding. "Let it happen."

Let it happen.

He's okay with this. He wants this, too, on some level, to watch this god have his way with me where

Ben can't anymore. But this isn't just a proxy thing—
Ben and I figured out we're very capable of satisfying
each other.

But that's just it.

I wasn't satisfied the way *this* will be satisfying. Ben
is steady and sure and I know he'll see to my needs; but
Thor already feels like even though he's a god, he's the
one worshipping me, and I'm content to go limp and
let him.

My eyes flutter shut as I come up onto my toes and
press my lips to Thor's. His hand goes to my throat,
pinning me against him, and he takes his time tasting
my mouth—his tongue laps at mine, his lips pressing
delicately to the corners of my mouth, the edges,
the top.

We're moving, walking backwards; I feel something
soft against the backs of my legs and Thor uses his hold
on my neck to lower me flat onto my back across Ben's
makeshift bed. It's more than big enough for the two of
us and my arms stretch wide, pushed there by Thor's
insistent prodding. I let him position me, mold me, my
mind sighing in relief to have someone else take
control.

Every moment of the past few months has been
nothing but *thinking* and *planning* and *doing*—I need
someone else to make the choices. I need someone else
to tell me what to do.

"Take her clothes off," says Ben behind us. His voice

is strained, and I slit my eyes open to see his cock in his hand as he gives it long, slow strokes.

Thor buries his face into the crook of my shoulder, his teeth and lips alternating their way down the slope of my neck. He props back on his knees to hook the edge of my shirt in his fingers. I shift up and it pulls off easily, and he disrobes me, sure, steady movements that he intersperses with kisses to my stomach, my knees, my thighs.

There, he stops, positioned between my spread legs, and the look on his face is all wonder, all awe as he stares down at my pussy. He whispers something in a language I don't know—Asgardian, maybe?—before casting a look at Ben.

He's waiting for orders. For permission.

My body is a riot of relaxation already, every muscle gone to effervescence at these small tasks of being cared for; and the moment I realize that Thor is letting himself be controlled by Ben, a surge of desire burns through me. I see it reflected in Ben's eyes, the pupils dilating, darkening.

"Lick her pussy, Thor," Ben says. "Make her come. Twice."

"With just my tongue?" Thor asks and juts his chin at something across the room.

I start to rise up to see what it is when Thor pushes me back down with a chastising grin.

"Ah-ah, no peeking. Ben?"

"Get it. Pump it in and out of her pussy. She can take it all."

What?

I'm not given a second to think about it — Thor hurries across the room and returns, but I dutifully stay flat on the bed.

Something presses against my folds. Something hard but smooth, and then Thor nuzzles his face into my cunt with a snarl more beast than man and I rock backwards, gasping.

He wastes no time; his tongue lashes out, fighting through my folds, finding my clit with expert precision, and there he lingers, lapping it forcefully. Whatever is pressing against my pussy lips pushes deeper, entering me, and I cry out and buck beneath him.

"Hold her down. She needs this," comes Ben, but his voice is at the edge of my awareness, all my focus drawn to the space between my legs, to the god currently sucking on my clit and whatever he has that's now slowly pumping in and out of me.

I buck again and Thor's arms come up to brace against my hips.

"Play with her tits," Ben orders. "I want to see her nipples squeezed."

Thor lets one hand wander higher, higher, until he palms my breasts, and he snarls again, a rumble of desire.

"How does she taste?" Ben asks.

"Her taste," Thor purrs into me, "is sweeter than nectar. I will never tire of this."

It's like I'm not even here. It's like they're discussing me in the next room.

I fucking love it.

Thor runs a long, slow lick from my ass all the way to my clit, darting around the toy he's still using to pump in me, savoring each stop along the way, the dips of my labia, the heat of my entrance.

My mind heaves, whirls, deliciously swarmed with sensation and the unraveling of being at someone else's mercy.

"Make her come," Ben states, decisiveness in his voice that has me stumbling toward the edge, desperate, sweating with need.

Thor's hand tweaks my nipples, rolling the pebbled nubs between his fingers, and I buck again, helpless, my climax building as he returns to my clit and licks passionately now, alternating the licks with faster and faster thrusts. He drags the flat of his tongue over my clit, over, and over, nursing my first orgasm from me—he's bringing it on stronger, harder, faster, his fingers twisting my nipples with just enough gentle pressure, the toy thundering in and out of my pussy.

I come with a bright scream, the orgasm ripping up from my cunt and flooding through my body, a lightning crack in a storm, a wave rising high. Shudders make my limbs twitch and tremble, and I expect Thor to pull back now, to give me a beat to recuperate—

"Another," Ben says. "One more."

Thor pulls his arm down and presses it across my cunt, holding me down with the force of his palm. He uses two fingers to spread my labia and lift my hood, exposing my swollen, raw clit to him.

"Daisy," he murmurs. "Fall apart, goddess; I shall catch you."

He licks my clit, just once, and it's so sensitive still that I scream again, body involuntarily jerking against the sensation. But he holds me firm, one hand on my pussy, the other still pumping the toy, keeping my pleasure ever building.

My eyes find Ben, slowly stroking himself, and he watches me with a knowing, feral smirk. He knows how sensitive I am after just one orgasm; he knows, also, how powerful a second one is, but how much I fight through the stimulation to get there.

"Thor—" I gasp. "Ben—"

Thor licks my clit, faster, faster, and I arch backwards on the bed, biting my lips together, willing myself not to scream, to just accept this, to trust that Ben and Thor know what I need better than myself. And, *oh*, the desire that rises up through the overstimulation, the quick welling of pleasure that Thor demands out of my body with his punishing tongue. He angles the toy up, hitting my G-spot, and I see stars.

The second orgasm breaks over me, and if I screamed before, now I *wail*. The mix of pleasure and need and too sensitive and not enough is a war that explodes through me, soothing every muscle, erasing every worry. There is only here, now, this wondrous moment, stars pricking my vision, my body used and worshipped and sated.

I'm limp with release, my head lolling to the side, so I see Thor peel up, grinning, his chin wet with my juices.

He pulls out the toy he'd used to fuck me with.

It's his hammer. The handle of his hammer, to be exact, and it's now just as drenched as his chin, thoroughly coated in my wetness, and he runs his tongue down the shaft, eyes rolling shut.

"Mm, Daisy," he moans, and I writhe under him, already needy again, already undone.

"You both did so well," Ben tells us. "Now, Thor—"

It isn't over?

Of course it isn't.

Thor eyes Ben and nods, grinning wide. He sets aside the hammer and pulls off his tunic to reveal his naked body.

I'd suspected he'd be massive.

I did not expect he'd be nearly comparable to Ben in his current form.

The size of Thor's dick has me shooting up onto my elbows, equal parts desire and fear jarring through me. It's not just long, but thick, hard as steel and lined with rigid veins.

"Ben?" I question, chest rising in jerky breaths.

"You can take it, Daisy," Ben says. "You need this. Just relax. Let us take care of you."

But I know from the added surge of wetness in my pussy that he's right.

I not only need this. I want this.

My eyes climb up Thor's body—the tight V of his hip muscles, his chiseled abs, his truly staggering biceps and shoulders—to find a patient, admiring smile on his face.

He bends down, crawling over my body until I lie flat again.

"Trust me, Daisy," he tells me, and behind him, I see Ben stroking his hard cock faster now, his mouth forming the same words. *Trust me.*

So I pull Thor down to me in a kiss, and I do.

12

THOR

Daisy lays on her back, lust-heavy eyes warm and soft. Her body is completely open to me, legs spread, perfect cunt dripping and aching for me. My cock throbs in desire.

Nearby, Ben watches, eyes heavy and lidded.

On my knees, I run my palms over her body, letting my fingers drape loosely against her skin. Daisy positively *ripples* with pleasure under my touch.

I stop at her hips, my fingers pressing into her firm flesh, gripping her. Daisy blinks up at me, heavy-lidded. Open.

Waiting to be filled.

My hands tighten on her hips, lifting her body up. She willingly lets me shift her body, turn her around on her hands and knees so that her ass is up toward me. I stroke her back, my touch feather-light, and she shivers again.

I am on my knees, too, as I should be, a devout worshipper of her body. My cock aches for her, and with her ass and pussy so perfectly poised before me, I cannot help but rub my head along her moist entrance.

She moans, the sound nearly undoing me.

"Ben," I say, nodding at the beast of a man.

He looks up at me, eyes wide. He did not expect to be involved.

I know neither of us wants the other, but we *both* want Daisy—and she wants *both* of us. I cup her ass, part her cheeks, and run my finger against her entrance there. She moans, her mouth popping open with an audible, wet *smack*.

Ben's cock dribbles with hot pre-cum at the sight of her mouth, open wide. I nod at him, and he moves closer, dropping to his knees in front of her, cock first. Daisy's eyes are shut as I rub my finger along the edge of her asshole, applying pressure. It's like a lust button; I push against it, and she moans again.

Ben's heavy, huge cock rubs along Daisy's jawline, and I know that she's surprised by the wet warmth dripping over her. But she turns, arching her back so that she leans against my finger at her ass while also opening wide, running a tongue along Ben's monstrous penis. His balls retract and so do mine, both of us responding to the way she pleases us, just by being her, just by accepting us.

My cock will no longer be denied. I still play with her ass using my fingers, but Daisy's legs are spread so wide I easily notch my cock against her entrance. She's slick and hot, her body ready for me, aching for me.

I slide inside, and she moans against Ben's penis, her head bending down as her tongue lathes him. Her back arches up, and I use some of her own dripping moisture to lube my finger's entry into her ass, playing with her as I stroke inside her cunt with my penis.

A finger in her ass, my cock in her pussy, Ben's head against her lips—we fill her every hole.

And she is *loving* it.

There are so many thoughts in that pretty head of hers, it takes two cocks and my fingers to silence them. But now that we are here, her body a bridge between ours, she easily slips into a rhythm. Daisy leans back, her pusy clenching around my cock, her legs spread so wide that she takes all of me in, all the way to the hilt. Then she pulls away, her tongue gliding along Ben's cock.

Grunting, Ben leans down, cupping Daisy's swinging breasts and holding her up with his massive arms. With her hands now free, Daisy grips his cock—it takes both of her hands to wrap around the massive penis, and she slides her tongue across the top, followed by her tight grip up and down his shaft.

I shift my hands from her ass to her hips, helping to support her more and get a better angle of her pussy against my cock. Her legs go limp—I support her whole lower half with my hands, lifting her body and slamming it into my cock. Ben holds her chest—there is no part of Daisy on the ground, the two of us support her body, gliding her over my cock, then his, then hers.

Gripping her hips, I feel the shaking of her orgasm. Her pussy clenches around my cock, her cunt quivering. I steady her, driving my cock into her harder, harder, as her body bucks up over nothing but air. Ben's hold is strong, too, and we keep her steady as her entire body spasms around both of our cocks. I release into her sweet, hot pussy, slamming her body down on top of my cock so forcefully that I lean back, my own ass against my legs, her naked body bouncing upon my hips.

With a roar, Ben releases his load, a hot shower of white cum spraying up, dousing Daisy's body, dripping over her taut nipples and down her flat stomach.

My cum fills her body; his cum paints her skin.

I ease Daisy off my cock, letting her slide down the length of me and collapse on the bed. She melts into a liquid pool of spent desire, boneless and limp and utterly, utterly, *utterly* satisfied.

13

DAISY

Thor helps me into the shower just off of Ben's room—it's one we retrofitted for him, so it's massive. The water steams the air quickly but Thor is efficient, cleaning every inch of my body with the same tender veneration he showed earlier. I can't help the soft moans that come, my very soul in a happy, relaxed fog, and by the time I'm clean, my arms come around Thor's neck, and my lips find his.

I want to tell him thank you. I want to explain how I can't remember the last time my shoulders weren't tense or I felt truly satisfied. But I can't get the words to form—a snap of guilt keeps them in my throat.

"He did these things for you, too, Daisy," Thor whispers against my lips. "He was as much a part of it as we were. It was all of us."

How did he know? How can he tell already exactly what's troubling me?

I arch up into his embrace, kissing him with the last vestiges of my energy. I feel his cock stir between us and it cuts my lips into a grin.

"Ah-ah," he chastises and pulls back to plant a kiss on my nose. "You need rest now, I think. And something to drink."

"Unfair." I pout, but he just adjusts me to carry me in his arms.

We step out of the bathroom and Ben has a stack of towels waiting. They both alternate drying me, and I'm all too happy to let them, unable to get the goofy smile off my face.

"She looks better," Ben says and eyes Thor with a sly smile. "Good job."

"To you as well," Thor tells him, a weird sense of camaraderie passing between them, and I giggle, because this is just *weird,* isn't it?

But so, so good.

I DRESS, I drink enough water to Thor and Ben's satisfaction, and I even eat a little more—then it's back to the lab, despite my body already thrumming to rip off my clothes again. Now that I know what's possible, what I can have again, all I want is to tumble back into bed with Thor and Ben and go utterly numb with ecstasy.

It sure as hell beats reading over the data from my

testings, still no fucking closer to knowing what I should do for the first gem device prototype.

I have samples of most known metals, and I've been running the composition of each of them through simulations since I got the gem back yesterday. But nothing has proved conclusive—a few are ranking high, but not enough that I feel comfortable risking Ben and the gem in a test. Even tungsten, iridium, and fucking *sterlinium* aren't holding up to where I'd like the data points to be — all of them on their own would likely shatter before Ben could channel any energy out of the gem.

I could make a blend of metals, but I have so little sterlinium, and it's not exactly like I can pop down to the store and buy more. I can *steal* more, but I'm sure Heroes Org is on full alert since my break in at the crash site. Could Thor get me more? It's too risky— he'd have to tell his brother what's going on, why he's taking sterlinium, and I'll be damned if Ben and I end up back under Heroes Org's thumb.

I gotta start somewhere, though. Maybe tungsten mixed with iridium. A small amount. I can run some tests—

Movement pulls my focus away from the lab table. Thor sits on a stool, one elbow propped on a table, chatting casually with Ben while they take turns casting looks at me, like they're keeping an eye on me.

They are, I realize.

My chest warms and I grin stupidly—

My eyes fall to the hammer at Thor's feet. He's cleaned the handle, but still, my grin widens.

A thought occurs to me, and I launch up from my chair. "What's your hammer made out of?"

Thor gets a look on his face that's first curious, then horrified. "I—I would gladly make sacrifices necessary to stop Niberu, but my hammer—"

"No, I mean—well, it'd be *nice*, but I wouldn't ask that of you." I wink at him. "I meant—it's not of this earth. Its composition might give me a better clue as to what kinds of alloys will best support the gem, since that isn't of this earth, either."

Thor's eyebrows shoot up. Without hesitation, he stands and picks up the hammer. It lays down on my table with barely a sound, and the way he handles it makes it look light as air—but the moment I try to pull it closer to my analyzer, it won't budge.

I give him a helpless look.

He bows his head. "Only the worthy shall—"

"Yeah, yeah, I know the myth. Doesn't make it less insulting, though. Can you move it over like an inch? Thanks."

I settle back in as the machine whirrs, a laser running over the top of Thor's hammer. I expect it to take awhile—it's *alien metal*, after all—but in a few seconds, my computer beeps.

Which means I have every metal in this hammer on file.

My hand shakes as I pull up the results. I don't

know why—I've run dozens, hundreds of tests over the past few months. Why is this one different?

But it is. I can feel it.

The test results flash across my screen.

"Sterlinium, osmium, and—" I blink, lean closer, read it again. "Moon dust? Seriously?"

I throw Thor a confused frown.

He shrugs. "I didn't form it. It was forged in the heart of a star by the most trustworthy, skilled craftsmen of our galaxy."

My mind tumbles to a halt. "Who made the Crown of Arathustra?"

"It has no known maker. Some say it came into existence with time itself."

"Helpful. But—" I run a finger down the length of Thor's hammer.

If whoever made this impressive piece of alien weaponry put these three very obtainable metals into it, then it's likely—*possible*—that similar metals were used in the Crown of Arathustra, which means I can totally make a brace that'll support the gem.

I clap my hands together and turn on Ben and Thor with a huge smile. "All right, boys, it's time to get to work."

14

THOR

I watch Daisy work.

At first, my bemused gaze is merely an appreciation of both her body and her mind, working in harmony. She is both efficient and focused, her movements from laptop to microscope to spectrometer as elegant as the most graceful dancer.

But watching her single-minded focus reminds me of other great minds.

My thoughts drift to sorrow and darkness.

In Asgard, we knew Niberu was coming. We knew he would bring a reign of terror and destruction, and even though he arrived with his daughter, Rora, and the pretense of peace, we knew.

We knew.

No one with the Crown of Arathustra comes with peaceful intentions.

My mother led the research. She was not only a

most benevolent queen of Asgard; she was a genius. And more than that, she was wise. There is a difference between intelligence and wisdom, and my mother had both.

But in the end, it didn't matter.

My mind casts back to that last day. I do not wish to relive the memory—I have far pleasanter things to think on, recent events reveling in pleasure. Yet I seem unable to think of anything else.

That last day, after my sister had discovered the treachery of Niberu, I stole the gems he had collected. It did little good—he still utterly destroyed Asgard—but we at least damaged him in the process.

My sister—known as Hela, then—had taken one and disappeared. The goal was always to do as much damage as possible to Niberu. He was an impossible foe to fight, but if we divided his power, separated it…

"You take the other. Flee. Hide," Hela had told me as I clutched the gem—bright blue and sparkling—in my hand. I could feel its power radiating.

It was intoxicating.

I watched Hela escape with her gem.

And I…

Gods save me, I…

I wanted to fight. And I had in my hands the means to do so.

Here is the truth I have told no one.

I was supposed to take the power gem I had stolen from the Crown of Arathustra and *hide* it.

Instead? I used it.

I know. I *know*. The power is too much—it should not be used. It should never be used. No one being should *ever* wield that much power, even if it's done in an attempt to protect his home planet, in a hope to save those he loves and fight evil.

Power corrupts.

I was not fool enough to put the gem in my own body. Instead, I placed it in my hammer, affixing it into the metal. And then I wielded the weapon, intent on using it to *obliterate* Niberu as a threat.

It was my rage that ruined it.

Had I been pure of heart, perhaps…perhaps that would have made the difference. But while I had noble intentions, I was also berserk with blood lust. As monstrous as Ben in the form of the Wreck.

The power filled my veins, electrified my muscles, blacked-out my mind.

I wanted nothing more than to destroy…

Everything.

Here is the shame of my heart.

Not all the destruction of Asgard lay in Niberu's hand.

It was I who smashed through the castle roof, a blur of furious power.

It was I who cracked the floor, breaking the tile mosaics as I stormed to him.

It was I who broke the throne my father sat on, the one destined for me, I who smashed my powered hammer through the gold and watched the pieces skitter across the rubble, I who, in a blind rage, smashed through the wall behind it, through the laboratory, leaving nothing but destruction in my wake as I sought out Niberu.

I found, instead, my mother.

She was already dying. That is my only solace. It was not I, in my blind rage, who killed my mother.

I had come too late.

"My child," she whispered through cracked and bleeding lips, her body stained black with plasma burns.

The power raged over me, a fury of flames coursing through my body.

Death. Hate. Revenge. Smash. Kill.

Those were the words the power gem whispered into my soul, blinding me to all else.

But my mother—

She whispered other words.

Love. Safe. Calm. Peace.

Here is the only solace of my soul.

My mother's voice was stronger than that of the power gem.

My fury abated.

The power subsided.

And when I looked at her, death rattles shaking her broken body, I was able to pull out of the influence of the gem.

Her love brought me out of the corruption.

And as she watched, too weak from her injuries to move, I ripped the gem from my hammer.

"That is not you," she whispered. "My darling son. You are not the fury. Do not bow to that."

She gasped, choking on her own blood.

"You are meant for greater things than destruction."

Those were her dying words.

Around me, Asgard burned.

I found my brother. I gave him the gem. Little Loki, the trickster, the clever one.

I trusted him more than I trusted myself.

"Never let me have that gem," I warned him. "Hide it from both Niberu and me."

And he had.

I BLINK, coming out of my reverie. Daisy's brow is furrowed in frustration as her formulas do not produce what she wants.

I was not able to save my own home.

I shall do all I can to help her save hers.

This plan of Daisy and Ben's—it could work. The gem filled me with rage, but the Wreck is already so primal; perhaps it will not affect him the way it did me.

Perhaps we have a chance.

15

DAISY

IT TAKES A FEW DAYS TO RUN TESTS ON THE SUPPLIES I have to determine if I have enough to craft a brace that'll fit Ben, so I split my time between tinkering with my machines and getting absolutely *railed*.

The difference between now and even just a week ago is astounding. A week ago, I was so stressed and terrified that I could hardly function outside of my work, and Ben was too — now, both of us *smile*. Like a *lot*. Thor does, too, and I get the feeling that he naturally smiles a lot, though he was somewhat like us before we started this menage—sullen, afraid, the weight of the world on his shoulders.

Has Thor been the missing piece the whole time? Not only in mine and Ben's relationship, but in my work as well. The data he provided with his hammer and his stories of the Crown of Arathustra is invaluable.

I couldn't do any of this without him.

And as I lay on Ben's massive bed one night, Thor's hand on my bare stomach and Ben's chest at my side, I wonder how long this can last. I feel like we're tempting fate too much to indulge in this goodness— Thor fucking me at Ben's commands, Ben participating as he's able. Am I selfish to keep this going? But every session is Ben's idea, and I can't deny how much happier he is now too.

Maybe this isn't just a fling. Maybe I can keep them both—my boys—even after we finish this brace and defeat Niberu.

A moan bubbles in my gut and I twist onto my side, burying myself against Thor's chest. He shifts, half asleep, and pulls me to him, and I listen to the rumble of his breathing inflate and deflate his massive chest.

After we defeat Niberu.

As if it'll be that simple.

As if, in the chaos of fighting the strongest force in the universe, I might not lose Ben, or Thor, or them both.

Fuck.

Really, deeply *fuck*.

I've run the test four times today alone and still, the data flashes up at me.

I don't have enough sterlinium to make the brace for Ben. Not enough that'll meet the percentage

LIZA PENN & NATASHA LUXE

requirements to even come close to matching the composition of Thor's hammer. I've run simulations with other comparable metals, but it has to be sterlinium, and it has to be *more* sterlinium than I have even if I melt down every speck of it in this bunker.

Fuck fuck *fuck*.

Thor finds me at my lab table, typing away at my computer. I feel Ben behind us, watching, always watching.

I type faster, flicking a stray hair behind my ear.

Ben and Thor share a look. They can communicate about me wordlessly now.

It's annoying.

It's amazing.

I hate how much I've come to depend on the pair of them, like I need two godlike men to sustain me.

But I do. I really do.

Thor comes up behind me and starts kneading my shoulders. "You did not sleep well, Daisy?"

I melt back into his touch. God, his *hands*—how is someone as large as he is so good with his *hands*? He could have been a masseuse in another life, his deft fingers instantly finding my sorest muscle and massaging it into submission.

"I wanted to get a head start today," I lie and, reluctantly, I stand, pulling out of his touch.

"She's lying," Ben says.

I glare at him. "Screw you, all right? Can I just have one second to be *human* amongst you *gods*?"

Ben's face dips, but he doesn't react to my banter. "What's wrong?"

Thor has his hand on my wrist. He watches me, patient, and I sigh.

"I don't have enough sterlinium. I have to break into Heroes Org again. Or—or find some crash site I haven't scavenged yet, but that's unlikely, and their security measure are going to be through the *roof* now, and—"

"Daisy," Thor moans my name, reaching up to cup my face. "You have me now. I will contact my brother, and—"

"No." I shake my head, hard, and over Thor's shoulder, I see Ben tense. "No, we aren't working with Heroes Org. Anything they get their hands in becomes *theirs*, and I don't trust them to not misuse Ben, or the gem, or—" Or *me*, I think, but I don't say that.

Thor bites the inside of his cheek. He's so close to me that I can smell the musk of him, a delicious, delirious buzz floating through my panic.

"What if," he starts, "there was another contact I could connect you with?"

I sip in a breath. "Who?"

"My sister. Persephone."

My brain shudders to a halt. "The—*Villain Queen* Persephone? *That* Persephone?"

Thor nods.

"She's your sister—so she's also a—"

"Her name on our planet was Hela."

"Holy shit." My eyes go to Ben, who shares my look of shock mixed with horror mixed with —possibility?

Will a Villain Queen help us? Or will she seek to use us just like Heroes Org?

What choice do we have?

The satellites haven't shown Niberu enter our galaxy yet, but he will, soon. The riots across the country—across the *world*—have only gotten worse, people driven to a frenzy over the proof of alien shit going down.

I can't go to Heroes Org. I can't waste time scavenging crash sites.

"Okay," I whisper, leaning into Thor's touch. I rise up and hook my arms around his neck, letting him hold me, and immediately, I feel myself breathe. A real, deep, cleansing breath. "But Ben's staying here," I say to Thor, to Ben. "And we aren't telling her *what* the sterlinium is for, okay? We'll just trade for it. I have some tech she might be interested in."

Thor hums against me. "Whatever you need, Daisy. I'll set it up."

Thor and I leave the bunker before he generates a portal, and when we step through, we're in a tropical paradise.

Because of course the lair of the most powerful super villains in the world would be in a fucking *trop-*

ical paradise. I mean, what did I expect? An icy tundra in Siberia? Who the fuck would want to stay there.

Thor sets off up a path towards a legit *castle*, and I stumble along behind him, my mouth gaping open. We enter easily, something over us beeping, acknowledging our presence, but I get the feeling Persephone knew we were here the moment we stepped through.

Groups of people pass us as we hurry through twisting halls. I think I recognize some of them from the news, various Villains that Heroes Org's Heroes have dispatched over the years. Part of me recoils— these are *villains*, after all—but they smile at us, friendly, and a few are laughing at something playing on a phone, and they're all just so *normal* that by the time Thor stops in front of a door, I'm almost not nervous anymore.

Almost.

Until I turn to face the door, and even the fucking *door* is intimidating, a massive mahogany piece of art carved with scenes from what has to be a battle. Likely one on Asgard, now that I know who Persephone really is.

Jesus fuck, what even is my life anymore.

Thor knocks. A beat, and the door opens on its own, showing a massive office done out in what can only be described as medieval chiq. Balcony doors open on the far wall let in sunlight and the gentle ocean breeze, softening what would otherwise be an overwhelming dark room.

Behind a desk in the center sits Persephone.

She's...stunning. Speechlessly stunning. The kind of effortless beauty that defines the very word *queen*, and when Thor enters, she rises from her chair, an emerald green dress rippling into position around her movements.

"Brother," she says. Her eyes flick behind him, to me, and her face tightens. "You have a guest. A guest who...knows quite a lot."

"Play fair, Persephone, I beg of you," Thor says, and I get the feeling there's something more going on in the silence that follows, one in which Thor and Persephone stare at each other, before Persephone sighs and bats her hand.

"Her mind is safe," she says, and I balk.

"My mind was *not* safe at some point?" I squeak. I know nothing about Persephone's powers, just that she's the single most terrifying, powerful entity in the world, and Heroes Org has been after her for decades.

Persephone gives me a flat smile. "What is this about? Could it have anything to do with the crash site you visited before promptly disappearing? Quite unlike you, Thor."

Thor, in front of me, clenches his hands into fists. I can't help it, reacting like a magnet, and I grab his wrist between both of my hands. What comfort can I possibly give this god? But he's nervous, I can tell. And that fact has me on high alert.

"I am not allowed my own business?" he asks. "I went to the site after Loki received reports of theft. There was none I could find. Daisy—" he nods at me. "—is a separate issue. We have come to make a request of you."

Persephone frowns. "You found no reports of theft, hm?"

Thor holds. I feel him shaking. Can she sense he's not telling the truth? He's really a shit liar.

"Yes," he says, but he might as well be screaming *LIES.*

Persephone narrows her eyes. After another long moment, she sniffs. "What *separate issue* has brought you to my humble home, brother?"

Thor slips his arm around my waist. "Daisy is a human scientist working on a project to protect other humans from Niberu's advances. We have the direct front covered, but Daisy's project will, I believe, add great value."

"Oh? And what is this *project*?"

"That is not necessary for what we need."

"Which is?"

"Sterlinium."

Persephone laughs. It's bright and cutting and makes me flinch.

I step forward. "I can pay you. Or—I can trade." I pull out the bag I'd brought with a few samples of my tech. "I have all sorts of devices. Security, weapons, improvement—"

Persephone cuts her hand up, and my lips snap shut.

"You come to me, asking for sterlinium, and you will not even tell me what it is for?" Her question is directed at her brother, as though I didn't speak at all.

Thor's face is grim. "Please, sister. Have I ever asked you for anything? Trust me."

Persephone comes around her desk. She stops just in front of Thor, eyeing him first.

Then she finally looks at me.

"You," she points at Thor, "have earned this request. You," she points at me, "have not."

"I can pay," I say again and hold up my bag. "What do you—"

"Not with tech." Her eyes zip back to Thor.

His face flares red, starting in his neck, rising up to his cheeks.

"You know what's coming," Persephone says to him, her voice lower, steadier. "You know what my powers need. This is the only thing I will accept."

"You have never asked this of me before," Thor stammers.

"Not you. Her. Just her."

"Would someone like to tell me what's going *on?*" I snap.

Persephone and Thor both look at me. And I suddenly regret saying anything at all.

If I thought being the sole focus of *one* god was intense — two is unwinding.

Persephone reaches up and curls a lock of my hair around her finger. I don't know why I let her; something palpitates off of her, electric, infusing.

"My price for sterlinium," she starts, "is for you to perform in my throne room."

"Perform?" I squint at Thor.

He's panting. Hard. Gasping, almost, and I recognize that reaction—he's aroused.

What the...

"Thor will explain." Persephone flips her hand at her brother. "Take her down and tell her what she will do. I'll be along in a moment."

THOR

WHEN WE GET IN THE ELEVATOR, DAISY WHIRLS ON ME. "Okay, explain," she demands. I can see a flush on her cheeks and the thrum of her pulse in her neck. She's worried and scared and...a little tantalized.

"First, you need to understand something about my sister," I say, unsure of how best to approach the situation. "She feeds off energy."

A pair of lines form between Daisy's brow as she concentrates. I want to kiss them away, but I know the gravity of the situation—and time is of the essence. "High emotion of any kind directly influences Persephone. If there is lots of violence, she becomes far more violent."

Daisy blanches, and I know she understands the issue. If Niberu comes—and he *is* coming—he will bring war and destruction. And he has no idea what kind of phoenix that will rise from the ashes of terror he brings.

"But good emotion—happiness, joy, satisfaction…" I cough. "Erm, sexual energy—those things enhance Persephone's power in a different way. A more, er, positive way. She also…" I look away. "She can sense the depth of your emotion. Your love shines through. It's not just about the sex, but the emotions behind it."

"You're telling me your sister gets high off other people having sex?" Daisy's voice raises with incredulity.

"When you put it like that…"

The elevator door opens, and I step into the corridor. A few short steps and we're at a door on the ground level. "Just…try to keep an open mind. And know that this is for the sterlinium."

I open the door.

To Persephone's sex dungeon.

Daisy's eyes grow wide as she sees the myriad of Heroes and Villains throughout the wide room. Some booths are open, tilted so the people inside them are on view. Others are more private, closed off so that we can see nothing but can hear the erotic moans from within. A bar on one end holds a host of people, not all human, drinking and flirting and pleasuring themselves or others.

But the most obvious, cannot-be-denied element of the room was the stage. A man wearing nothing but a cloak stands in the center of the stage, portals open in whirling circles around him. He walks from portal to portal, sucking a cock through one, fingering a pussy through another, playing with beads and dildoes, cracking a whip, and more. He moves languidly by each of the portals he controls, as if this play is nothing more than an idle pastime, but his satisfied smirk is evident even from the back of the room.

As Daisy and I walk forward, the man—known as the Doctor—finishes up with each of his willing and eager participants.

Daisy grips my arm. "Wait—are we going on stage?"

I pull her to the side. "You are," I say. "Not me. Persephone feeds off high emotions, but even she would not want those sorts of emotions from her own brother."

"I—alone?"

I wait for her to focus on me fully. "Only if you want to," I say. "I know Persephone caged this as the trade for sterlinium, and I know she'd follow through with the deal, but you don't have to. Consent is a part of pleasure. If you don't willingly wish to participate, then you don't have to at all."

"I'm sorry—I just can't wrap my head around this." Daisy looks around at the various being in the room. It's a force to be reckoned with certainly. Scarlet stands to one side, using her mesmer powers to enhance everyone's pleasure—and likely drive more directly to my sister. Lillith and Fallon are nearby, Fallon hovering over top of her as he eats her out.

"That's a Heroes Org agent!" Daisy hisses at me. Piper—formerly Agent Carson—looks up from the booth, having heard her. She gives Daisy a salacious wink as both Ari and Bryce pleasure her. It reminds me, a bit, of how Ben and I both worship Daisy.

"It may seem strange—" I start.

"It seems fucking *awesome*," Daisy says. "When do we start?"

I laugh at her enthusiasm. Perhaps, since she's so better able to work when she's sexually relaxed, it's not that hard for her to see how Persephone takes that to a higher level.

"Well, I was thinking," I say, eyeing the Doctor as he descends from the stage. I motion him over. "I know that we don't want Persephone to see—and potentially use—Ben and his force," I whisper to Daisy. "But what do you think about him playing along from a distance?"

Her eyes widen, and she nods eagerly. She gets her cell phone out to text Ben about this new development as I explain the situation to the Doctor.

Daisy tentatively mounts the stage after a few minutes. I nod eagerly to her, and the Doctor waves his hands. A shimmering portal floats in the air before Daisy.

I squint. I can almost see movement behind it. Around me, I notice that many of the patrons have sat up, taking notice of this new person on stage, the singular—but large—portal before her.

The dark portal grows a bit. And then from within it emerges…

The most enormous cock any one in the room has ever seen.

Ben is able to keep his identity—and his location—hidden while still being present for Daisy's debut in Persephone's throne room. Since I feel wrong participating for my own sister, this enables Daisy to please herself *and* Ben *and* everyone in the room.

I feel my own cock harden. This will be a test for me as I refrain from participating. Denying myself pleasure has always been difficult, but I see it now as a uniquely delicious challenge.

Daisy looks from the stage out into the audience—to me. I give her an encouraging nod. She wasn't asking for permission—she is the one in charge of both Ben and me—but my approval seems to be all she needs to relinquish the last of her inhibitions.

Ben's cock is easily the size of my arm, bulging and hard, vividly purple and straining with veins. The enormity of it would make some people shy away, but not Daisy. She cannot fit the head in her mouth, much less his whole cock, but she runs her tongue up the side, lapping at it like it was made of candy.

Daisy alternates between licking his cock, tonguing his head, and stepping back to slowly undress, one article of clothing at a time. She lets her garments flutter to the floor as if they were flower petals, and the ease with which she moves makes me strain against my own clothing. I want to rip everything off my body, toss her on the ground, and fuck her senseless.

All around me, people are playing with themselves or others, in tune with Daisy's languid movements over Ben's hard cock.

But not me.

I deny myself not only an orgasm, but even a touch. My hands bunch into fists.

The Doctor, beside me, is equally hard, but he can control portals with one hand pumping his own cock, apparently. "Watch this," he mutters. He twirls his fingers.

On stage, Daisy whoops in surprises as her body floats up. It's as if gravity gives way; she moves through the air as if it were water.

It takes her a moment to figure out the dynamics of this new elements, but soon enough she wraps her legs around Ben's hard cock and anchors herself to him. She rubs her tits on either side of his cock, pressing them together so her breasts form a sheath around his dick.

Daisy wraps her legs around the base of Ben's cock—the only thing visible of him, thanks to the portal, although we can all hear his moaning. She coils her whole body around his cock, weightless with the Doctor's help, and moves up and down. The movement is sinewy, almost cat-like, as she roves over his penis, her luscious breasts gliding along his shaft.

When she leans back, we can all see Ben's pre-cum slicking over Daisy's skin, drenching her whole body, glistening. She stretches out her legs. It would be impossible for him to penetrate her, but she uses her fingers to open her slit wide. She, too, is slick and moist, her body eager for more.

She opens herself as wide as she can, then runs her pussy, hot and wet, over Ben's enormous shaft. I can tell from the way her body shivers, from the way her eyes roll up in her head, that she's moving so that her clit runs along his cock. She leaves a trail of her own moisture along his dick.

I groan—I can't help it. My own hard-on is aching, and I want nothing—*nothing*—more than to pound into her.

But I won't take this moment away from her, from Ben. This is *their* moment, their love on display for the entire world to see, their passion coming to fruition with the aid of portals and creative thinking,

Unable to bear it any more, Daisy slides a finger into herself. I see her thumb working frantically on her own clit, and I wish I could be the one sucking that orgasm from her pussy with my own lips. But it's enough to see it.

Ben erupts with his own orgasm, great mound of cum shooting up and raining down on the stage. Daisy laughs with sheer delight, and several people in the audience, including the Doctor himself, actually applaud at the show. It takes a lot to impress this crew.

My cock is still pained and hard. But there's a triumph in that, too, in denying myself the orgasm I want.

It will be better when it's with her.

With them both.

17

DAISY

I'M IN SUCH A DAZE OF PLEASURE THAT I HARDLY NOTICE Thor scoop me off the platform. The portal flickers, then disappears, taking Ben's cock with it, and I giggle, driven to laughter by that sight, by what I just did, by my brain still being unable to wrap around the fact that a literal *god* is walking me to the side of the room where he sets me down and gently, tenderly, redresses me.

"Do you think that was enough?" I ask between fits of giggles.

Thor tugs my shirt back on and answers by way of a long kiss. His body pins mine to the wall next to a booth, out of sight of the rest of the room; the air here is thick with the smells of sex and arousal, even more so now that my performance seems to have...unleashed everyone. Somewhere, someone is screaming in pleasure.

A deep rumble thunders in Thor's chest. I arch up against him, and he lifts me, pinning me to the wall, his lips trailing across my face, down my neck.

"Daisy," he growls against me, sucking my skin into his teeth. "You were perfect. I'm mad with lust for you now—I would take you here, I would—"

He stops with a louder growl, a growl of frustration, and I echo it. His teeth, his touch, his lips—all of it reignites my drive, my pussy clenching around empty air, needing to be filled. Getting off on Ben was satisfying, but I still *need*, I still *want*, and now that I know how well Thor can fulfill those extras *needs* and *wants*, I'm insatiable.

I moan and reach between us to grab his cock through his tunic. He hisses and growls again, nipping at my collarbone.

"Not here. Let us get that sterlinium so I may take you back to the lab, and there, Daisy, I promise, I will ravish you utterly."

Oh fuck me. "Okay, yeah, that sounds like a plan." I'm breathless beyond belief. When was the last time I *could* breathe, actually? Before Thor swept into my life, I think.

Thor sets me on the ground, grabs my hand, and the two of us book it, *fast*, across the throne room. I realize as we go that I didn't see Persephone in the crowd—did she have to be present for my *good emotions* to infuse her? Did that even count? I hope it did. I hope it didn't. I'm already biting my lip and wondering when

I can come back as Thor hauls me out the door and back up to Persephone's office.

There, she sits at her desk again, or still, but she looks up at me and smiles. "Well done, Daisy Miles."

I grin at her and sway a little, anchoring on Thor's arm. "Um. Thanks?" I feel my cheeks heat. This is so—I mean, I just paid for sterlinium in *sex*— "So, is that...are we good?"

Persephone waves at a container against the wall. I hadn't even noticed it. The massive box has a simple enough latching device, and when I cross and open it, I see sterlinium inside. Enough—more than enough—to finish Ben's brace.

I whip a smile back at Persephone. "Thank you."

"Thank *you*, Daisy Miles." She bends to read something on her desk. But she pauses, and her eyes go back to Thor, and the look she gives him is heavy suddenly, something unsaid passing between them.

"Only if you need to know," he tells her. More like *spits* at her, and before I can make sense of what just happened, Thor grabs my arm, lifts the container of sterlinium, and creates a portal back to my lab.

THOR TAKES me the moment we're back in my lab.

He makes good on his promise to *ravish me utterly*, and I'm all too happy to let him. Ben watches us with a lustful grin, but he doesn't get off on it this time—he seems appeased still from our performance, happy to watch as Thor rips my clothes off, tosses me on the bed, and slams home inside of me without pretense. I'm dripping for him; no need to waste time on foreplay. My head arches back and Thor pounds into me, a man on the edge, every muscle in his inhuman body strung taut.

When he's done, when he's seen to it that I've come twice more, he takes a cool washcloth and cleans me before dressing me again. Ben steadies me to my feet, and the two of them try to get me to rest or eat, but I can't—I'm all too tempted to just shuck all of my responsibility and stay here in this hidden bunker, getting fucked into oblivion.

But I have work to do.

I have a world to save.

Ben and Thor watch me work. I'm so used to both of their presences already that I hardly flinch at the intent way they stare at me, occasionally exchanging looks, whispering between each other.

It only takes a few hours. Too long, too soon, one of my alarms dings and I tap it silent as a shield slowly starts to rise out of my largest piece of equipment, the massive mold I designed. This mold did not come easily—I actually had to break into Heroes Org itself to get it. But damn, is it ever worth it—it can meld together the exact amount of metals I need to make Ben's brace in a fraction of the time I'd take to do it by hand.

I put on some gloves and reach into the machine to

remove the brace, but fuck, it's too big. I stumble to the side only for Thor to catch my hips and level me.

"Let me help, Daisy," he says and reaches for my gloves.

He's able to lift the brace easily. He holds it before himself, eyeing the design, the construction. Two giant crisscrossing arches will wrap around Ben's chest with a plate in the center for the gem.

"It's...ready?" Ben's voice is hesitant.

"Yes," I say, fighting for certainty. "I've run all the tests I can."

Ben blinks at me, his huge eyes round with shock. He swallows, hard, and nods.

Heaviness settles in my gut.

This is it.

We're going to test it. Like, *really* test it.

I want to mention how I'm not sure about the design of the brace and maybe I should take Ben's measurements again? I want to mention any of the dozen of worries racing through my head, but I just echo Ben's nod.

Thor holds the brace steady as I pull the gem out of the safe I'd stored it in. I don't dare touch it—I use a pair of tongs to transfer it into the brace's plate. It locks into place, and I swear the brace starts *humming*.

"Ideally," I start, needing to talk, needing to *move*, "the moment Ben puts it on, it should not only stabilize his condition—making him able to access the full breadth of his powers as the Wreck without losing control—but it should enhance those powers too."

Thor nods and slowly, *slowly*, crosses the room to Ben, like he's holding a live bomb. He kind of is. "And if it does not work?"

I can't think about that. "Just...put it on. Ben, lift your arms out."

He does. Thor slides the brace over Ben's head, up his outstretched arms.

The weight of the metal drops against Ben, settling tight between his pecks, the gem gleaming from the dead center of his chest.

"Ben?" I manage to gasp. "How do you...feel?"

Ben holds for a moment, his arms out, his head tipped down so he can stare at the gem.

I'm not imagining it. It *is* glowing, bright purple now, brighter and brighter—

"Ben?" Thor asks now, a hard twist in his voice. "What do you feel, brother?"

Brother?

Ben tips forward, catching himself on his hands, hard. It rattles the floor and I steady myself on Thor, the two of us rigid with watching Ben.

"Yes, indeed. How *do* you feel?"

The voice makes Thor and I whirl around.

And there stands Persephone. Her arms folded. Her dark eyes on Ben and the gem in the center of his chest.

Thor bellows and takes a threatening step towards

his sister, but all she does is hold up her hand, and he stops.

"What are you *doing* here?" he booms, and it makes my chest relax, just a little, knowing he *didn't* betray us.

Persephone waves at the now empty box of sterlinium. "Tracker. Of course."

Tracker? My mind trips. I scanned the box. I *did*—

But as I gape at Persephone, I have the sinking, stupid feeling that I underestimated her. That I trusted her a little too much, as Thor's sister.

Thor, too, seems gutted. "You *promised*—"

"The fate of all worlds is at stake. I make no promises, not even to you, Thor. Now." She looks up at Ben, who's still crouched over, who hasn't even seemed to realize we have a *guest*. "What is going on?"

A rumble shakes the room. It takes me a beat to realize it's *Ben*, growling.

"You can't be here right now," I tell Persephone, my focus half split between her and Ben. "You need to *go*."

"He is volatile," Thor explains. "We don't—"

Ben's growl grows louder, louder, until he's shouting, a primal tear of noise that yanks me to face him, everything trembling.

"*Ben*," I say his name as loud as I dare.

The moment I do, his head snaps up, dark eyes pinning on me, siting me like a hunter.

That gaze goes behind me. To Persephone.

Every hair on my body stands on end.

"Not Ben," the Wreck says from Ben's mouth. "*Angry.*"

18

THOR

FUCK.

That's the only thought in my head as the Wreck—not Ben—looks around the lab, eyes wild and feral in a way that makes me instantly aware that the gentle man I'd come to know is gone, hidden behind layers and layers of guilt and rage and fury.

His focus zeroes in on Daisy, who'd been calling his name.

Not his name. Ben's name. Because the Wreck is the monster who lives inside Ben's body, but it is not the same man.

It is not a merciful man.

It is a berserker, consumed with bloodlust.

And nothing else.

"Wreck!" the Wreck roars, both his name and his action. His massive hands turn into fists that he smashes into the wall, concrete crumbling. Daisy—

strong, interminable, capable Daisy—dashes outside his range, eyes wide in terror.

The Wreck turns at her movement.

I leap in front of him. Out of the corner of my eye, I see Persephone, watching. I know she could help—*she* knows she could help—but her help may very well kill Ben. And she's letting me try to save him.

He's a charging bull, blind to anything but the desire to destroy.

And Daisy is trapped in the corner.

I throw myself between them. It's all I can think to do, the only hope I have to stay the Wreck and stop the monster from tearing Daisy apart limb from limb. The Wreck slams bodily into me, and I hear both Daisy's scream and my own *oof* as the air is knocked from my lungs and I slam into the wall behind me.

Before the Wreck can make another move, I heave myself up. Panic flares in my mind—I have to protect Daisy, of course, but I also have to find a way to save Ben from himself. My sister does not need my aid, but if we are to prove to her that Ben is no monster, I have to stop him. Quickly.

It would be simple—to simple—to slam my hammer against the Wreck's head and end him forever. I know he's huge, monstrously strong, capable of more than I could ever imagine. But I also think it is absolutely possible to kill a beast.

But I can't kill Ben.

Somewhere in this time we've spent together, we

three have become irrevocably aligned. I may not feel sexual attraction toward Ben, but he's a part of my sexual attraction toward Daisy. And I cannot imagine a time with Daisy without Ben.

It's the three of us, or none of us.

Which means I have to save them both.

The Wreck charges at me again, fists swinging.

"Stop!" Daisy screams, but I know that her words can't penetrate the berserker rage hazing Ben's mind.

I know…

Because I've experienced it before.

I had hoped that Ben's primal, feral side would respond to the gem, but instead, it's filled him with more rage and fury than he can handle.

Before the Wreck can slam into me again, I leap up, flying at him. It's not enough to truly send him against the wall, but the force of my blow makes him skid across the tiled floor, putting at least some distance between him and Daisy.

"Ben—Ben, *listen to me*," I say urgently. If I can just reach the man inside the monster, I know—I *know* we can save him.

He picks me up as if I were a fly and flicks me across the room.

"Ben!" Daisy shouts, and this woman made of spit and fire runs *toward* the monster, not away. My body is aching, but I force myself, rushing quicker than she can to put myself between the Wreck and the woman.

This time, rather than go for the Wreck himself, I

aim for the brace and the gem. I shoot under his reach, hoping to rip it off his head, but the Wreck cannot be tricked that easily. He slams his arm against me, and I hurtle through the air, shattering the crystal spectrometer and sending rocks and glass and metal shards raining down over the lab.

"Ben!" Daisy screams.

The Wreck thunders toward her, footsteps making the floor shake. Daisy scrambles back.

The Wreck's nostrils flare. At the same time, I notice it, too—Daisy is bleeding, a heavy cut in her leg splattering the white floor with red blood.

"Daisy, watch out—!" I start, and then she slips in her own blood, tumbling to the floor. She scrambles back, back. For an instant, she slides far enough away from the Wreck's grip, under a heavy metal lab table, but then the Wreck lifts the table with his fingertips, tossing it away as if it weighed no more than paper.

I dodge the flying detritus and rush to the Wreck. He towers over Daisy's body, hunched against the wall, tears streaming down her face.

And then a portal opens behind Daisy.

Smooth, dark brown arms grab her from behind, yanking her away from the Wreck's swinging grasp. A second later, the portal re-opens on the other side of the room. Daisy and my sister stand there, Daisy's eyes wild as Persephone holds her.

The Wreck roars, turning around, and I lunge between them. "You're not getting to them, big boy," I say, and by all the gods of Asgard, I'm not sure if I'm enough to stop him while he's rampaging.

"Brother," Persephone calls, "I thought you said you had a good reason for getting sterlinium. I did not know you meant to use it to make a monster."

"Now isn't the best time for a chat, sister," I growl at the same time Daisy whacks Persephone's arm and shouts, "Ben is *not* a monster!"

But he's not Ben—not now. And another fear pierces my heart—my sister does not do well around the high emotions that violence evokes. I spare a glance behind her. Despite her light tone when speaking to me, I can see the tense way she carries her shoulders. She blames herself for this, and the guilt combined with the threat of terror is burning through her.

I suspect that it is only the love that Daisy feels for Ben, even in this form, that is keeping my sister's power balance in check.

"Is this your grand plan to defeat Niberu?" Persephone calls, her voice cracking.

"Yes!" Daisy whirls on her.

The Wreck slams both fists into the ground in rage, the tiles cracking.

"Okay, so it's not going so great at the moment," Daisy concedes.

The Wreck lunges—he has force behind him, but I have speed. I go for his neck. I'm nothing but a fly on the back of the beast, but he cannot immediately reach me.

"Brother—" I look into my sister's eyes at her pleading voice. I have known her my entire life, and I understand the look she gives me.

If you cannot contain the monster, I cannot help you.

I nod, then look to Daisy. I know my sister understands.

If I fail, save her.

She nods back at me.

Daisy could not have understood our silent communication, but as I struggle to wrestle the Wreck back, she whirls upon Persephone. "The power gem corrupts, we know that. We knew it before we began. But we can use it against Niberu. We *can.*"

I struggle, my muscles aching against the force that is the Wreck.

I cannot break the brace with the power gem around his neck.

Fighting will not work.

The Wreck cannot be injured, not in a way that would stop him.

Reason cannot work.

The gem overpowers his every thought, every action.

There is only one option left.

"Ben," I say, shutting my eyes to the monster and forcing my voice to speak only to the man. "Ben, this isn't you."

I use the words my mother used on me.

Only love can work in the face of the power gem's influence.

Love and hope and all things good.

What I feel—what I think Ben feels—is new. But what Ben and Daisy had together is not. "Listen to me, brother," I whisper in his ear as I cling to his back as the Wreck raises both fists, ready to smash them down on Daisy's delicate body. "You and I? We're not really here to fight. Not each other. Not even Niberu."

I can feel the hard coil in the Wreck's muscles, the tension that does not ease. But nor does he slam his fists against Daisy.

"Brother, we do not care for the fight. We care for the girl. *This* girl. We love her. We will not hurt her."

Those muscles are still tight, but his arms—his arms shake. I realize then that what the Wreck wants to do is *smash*, but Ben—Ben is fighting.

Ben heard me.

And slowly, his eyes fade back to *his* eyes. I feel his muscles settle. I don't let go, not yet, but I shift so I can see his face better..

"Ben?" I ask.

"Ben," he says, confirming, although his voice is still rumbly. Then he tilts his head. "And the Wreck. Both." His eyes focus on me. "Both. But...calm. I am in control."

19

DAISY

I RUSH FORWARD THE MOMENT THOR RELEASES BEN. THE two of them collapse to the floor, Thor on his knees, Ben propped up on his forearms — Thor immediately rushes back to Ben and gets there as I do, his eyes soft and tentative as he puts a hand on the back of Ben's head.

"Brother?" he prods.

I lay my hand next to Thor's, on the back of Ben's head. All the things he said to Ben vibrate on the air between us, and when Thor's eyes meet mine, I reach out with my other hand and touch his face.

Ben shifts, his massive shoulders rolling until he looks up at me.

His eyes are...different. Still *him*, but *more* in some way, settled instead of worried, resolved instead of tense.

"Daisy," he gasps. His focus goes up and down my

body, landing on the cut on my leg. "Oh, god—"

"It's all right." I twist to face him fully, putting my fingers against his cheeks. "I'm fine. Really. How are...you?"

He winces. Then he leans against my hands, turns, presses a kiss to my palm.

His eyes go to Thor.

"Thank you," he whispers.

Thor grins. He slaps Ben on the back. "Of course."

A throat clears.

The three of us twist to see Persephone, her lips pursed, fear still wavering in her eyes. To see this goddess reduced to mortal *fear* makes a tremor run through my body.

This is everything Ben and I fought to avoid for so long: discovery. I can already see the thoughts turning in Persephone's head, how she can use him, how she might—

"You did this," she starts, "to fight Niberu?"

I put myself in front of Ben. Me, bleeding down my leg, protecting a monster three times my size. "Yes."

She nods. Her eyes flick to Thor, back to me. "When you feel ready, come speak with me. I can offer what you are lacking."

"And what are we *lacking*?" I don't mean to spit the word, but it comes on the back of all Heroes Org's empty promises.

Persephone smirks. "Allies," is all she says.

My brows shoot up.

Allies.

It's been a helluva long time since we've had allies. But how can we trust someone who slipped in a tracker and followed us? Although...I'd totally do the same thing.

I hesitate. "We'll see."

Persephone bows her head. "Until next time, brother," she says, and with one last, genuine smile for me, a portal appears, and she's gone.

I hadn't realized I'd been holding myself so strong in her presence. The moment she leaves, every muscle in my body cries out in strain and my leg positively *aches*. I make a sort of whimper, and that's all Ben and Thor need before they set on me, swiftly coordinating so Ben holds me while Thor peels off my ripped pants. Ben grabs the first aid kit and Thor cleans my wound; Ben passes me a bottle of water and coaxes me to eat while Thor redresses me.

Together, the two of them get me onto Ben's bed, and yeah, okay, I definitely liked getting pampered, but I'm in no mood to sleep.

Thor presses two ibuprofen into my hand. "Take this, and rest."

I grab his wrist. "No. No way. Do you have any idea what we did today?"

Ben, laying out on his elbow next to the bed, smiles at my enthusiasm. The gem glows softly from the center of his chest.

As if I asked for demonstration—or maybe Ben's

just high on this success too—he throws his head back and *roars*. I've only ever heard him make that sound when he's lost in the Wreck, but he instantly bends back down, grinning.

"We did it." I pull on Thor's arm. "We *did it*. He's in control now, and when Niberu comes—"

My joy deflates.

"When Niberu comes," I say again, "we'll be ready for him."

Thor's smile pinches. I can see the doubt in his eyes.

He doesn't think Ben alone will be enough to fight Niberu.

Honestly, I never did, either. I never thought it'd just be Ben and I, alone on a battlefield. I always thought we'd find...allies.

I bite my lip. Maybe we should take a visit to Persephone. Maybe that wouldn't be so bad.

For now, though...

I toss back the ibuprofen, still holding onto Thor. The smile I give has pink heating his cheeks.

"Daisy," he says, his tone lifting. "You are injured. You need rest."

"Agreed," Ben says.

"I need to *celebrate*," I tell them. But I let go of Thor and lay back on the bed. Instead of obeying their insistences, I pull up the hem of the night shirt Thor got me to sleep in—I think it's one of his own tunics, actually —and run my fingers down the curly hair over my cunt.

"If you don't do something to help me feel good," I say, darting my eyes between Thor and Ben, "then I'll just do it myself."

Ben's eyes darken, a feral, predatory look overtaking him. But I don't fear it anymore—I still see *him* in there, and now that I do, that look has my pussy dripping, my belly squeezing with need.

Thor looks at Ben, helpless, his face and neck flushed with arousal. "What should I do, brother?" he asks.

Ben reaches one hand over. He gently brushes my stomach with his finger, sliding lower to part my legs, and when his fingertip comes up coated in my glistening juices, he groans.

"Suck on her nipples, Thor. Play with her breasts," he commands. "What our Daisy wants, our Daisy gets."

I squeal as Thor eases down over me, his lips immediately latching to first one nipple, then the next. Ben slides his finger back between my legs, his gentle, sure strokes against my wet lips and throbbing clit almost maddening in its slowness, but Thor matches Ben's pace. They'll draw this out, I know—they won't go fast, won't go rough, not until I'm healed.

The fact that I can do nothing but lay here and take whatever these two men choose to give me has my whole body going feather-light with euphoria.

War may be coming, but right now, I'm being worshipped.

20
THOR

THE PORTAL TO BRING BEN TO MY SISTER'S ISLAND IS perhaps the largest one I've ever made, and even then, Ben has to hunch to step out from the bunker laboratory onto the white, sandy shores of my sister's private base.

"Huh," Ben says, staring up at the castle. "Is that where—"

"Is it not familiar?" Daisy asks, grinning, giggling. I stifle my own smile.

"It's not like I *saw* anything," Ben said. "I just...felt..."

A deep purple stain washes over his cheeks. I feel my cock growing hard at the memory of Daisy riding his monstrous dick, suspended with magic and using portals to pleasure him.

"Focus," I say, my voice raspy.

"Right," Daisy replies, all efficiency. "We're here for

a purpose." She glances at me. "What's the purpose again?"

I smile indulgently. The truth is, I've not told either of them the full reason I had for bringing them here today. But I definitely don't need a Wreck-sized boner to distract anyone from the task at hand.

"This way," I say, gesturing them toward Persephone's castle.

It took some convincing to get both Ben and Daisy to see that joining forces with Persephone—and with Loki—would be to everyone's benefit. They understandably had some wariness when it came to Heroes Org, although they at least recognized that the treachery they faced came from the former head of Heroes Org, not my brother.

"As you know, my siblings and I have dedicated our lives to helping protect worlds from Niberu," I say. The three of us failed to protect Asgard—we will *not* allow that same level of destruction to befall Earth or any other solar system.

Daisy slips her hand in mine, squeezing my fingers in a comforting way.

"Niberu is a formidable foe," I continue. We crest the hill leading to the castle. Beyond, I can see the private villas my sister allows for guests, and I know that one has been reserved for the three of us.

"We can handle him," Ben says in his deep, rumbling voice.

I glance behind me, my neck craning up to get the full image of him. "I believe we can," I say. "Together."

The door to Persephone's castle opens with a puff of green smoke.

Loki stands on the other side, decked out in his garish green and gold. He has a smirk on his lips, some smart-ass remark no doubt ready, but his jaw hangs open when he takes in Ben. Ben has to bend over nearly in half to get through the oversized entry doors, but once inside, the vaulted ceiling enables him to stand fully and look down at my brother.

"I—well," Loki says. He raises an eyebrow at me. "I can see what you mean."

"And what do you see?" Daisy asks, ever on the defense.

Loki inclines his head to her, the only sign of respect he will give, I know. "I think your boyfriend more than confirms the old adage," he says in a pleasant, polite tone. "Size matters."

"It does," Ben adds. I can recognize the chuckle in his voice, but to my brother it sounds like menacing thunder. He swallows, paling a touch.

"Yes, well," Loki says, flustered. "This way."

Persephone had used a clever combination of architecture and portals to expand her throne room. The stage, usually reserved for sex and whatever other high emotions she can feed off of, is currently being used for its original purpose: a throne.

Made of black ebony and covered in golden silk, my

sister Persephone sits atop the huge throne, her head tilted back, watching as we enter. I stride into the room first, followed by Daisy, Loki, and then Ben. My eyes are on Persephone, but the room holds more than her.

It holds everyone we have gathered into our army.

There are still invisible lines. Fallon and Lillith are near Scarlet and Watcher, to Persephone's left. Behind them is an assortment of the beings with power—from Earth and not from Earth—who work directly for themselves or Persephone, earning them the title of Villain. To Persephone's right are the Heroes. All-American Man is chief among them, although Byrce, the Winter Warrior, is better suited on the other side. Gwen, my niece, smirks on the Steel Soldier's arm.

Hundreds of people crowd into the throne room.

They are an army.

A force to be reckoned.

All of their eyes drift past me and my brother, to the Wreck. To Ben. To the monster who wears the power gem in the brace on his chest.

"That'll do it," Steel Soldier says, appraising us with his eyes. "I mean, come on." He looks over the crowd, at the Heroes and Villains alike. "Niberu may be a big fucker, but he can't hold a candle to..." He gestures at Ben.

I'm not sure which is more impressive—the sheer size and obvious strength of the Wreck, or the fact that Ben is in control of a power gem, a task not even I could do.

Niberu is big, too, though.

And he has a gem of his own.

I look around the room, my eyes settling, finally, on my sister. I know her well.

There is fear inside her. Fear that we will not be enough.

But for the first time since Asgard fell, I also see hope.

"Niberu has strength," I say, letting my voice carry throughout the hall. "And he has a power gem of his own."

My words dull the emotions of the room.

"But," I say before the gloom can settle, "we have something he has never had."

Daisy steps forward. "We have allies!" she shouts. "We have each other!"

And the roar of triumph at that is deafening.

EPILOGUE: PERSEPHONE

OUR ARMIES ARE UNIFIED.

I allow them the joy this creates.

I allow them the hope.

But I cannot share in their revels.

As soon as the initial introductions and the celebrations that follow at our unified and powerful front are over, I slip away.

I feed off high emotion, and while sex is often the easiest way to get that emotional high, the dizzying array of emotional turmoil happening on this island is a gluttonous feast I do not care to gorge upon.

I go to my office. I go to the sterlinium-enclosed private room behind it.

The only place on this entire planet where I can feel silence.

Except…

It's not silence I find.

There is a whisper, too.

I stride across the barren room to the single table against the wall. To the enchanted and protected box on top of that table.

I lift the hinged lid.

Inside, nestled in silk, is a gem.

THE THIRD POWER GEM.

IT HAS BEEN mine since I stole it from Niberu. He paid for it with the blood of my people.

Rage washes over me, blinding me.

With shaking hands, I put the gem down, securing it in the box.

I have told myself for far too long that I would never—*ever*—use the stone. It is admirable that the monstrous being known as Ben and the Wreck can control the power gem in his brace.

I do not know if I could do the same.

It calls to me. It tempts me with its power.

It sings to me of the destruction I could reign upon the universe, a vast, devastating destruction that would make me Queen of Death for all to worship and be terrified of.

I leave the gem, the box, the room.

I CANNOT SUCCUMB.
Not.
Yet.

21

MORE

We want to thank you so much for sharing in this adventure with us! This book has been a labor of love, and it's made better by sharing with readers like you. Our newsletter will always keep you up-to-date with the latest sexy releases!

Keep reading for links to freebies and a sneak peek...

Please consider leaving a review—they help new writers more than almost anything else, and ensure that we can keep writing this series.

. . .

WANT to read more about Heroes & Villains? Sign up for our newsletter and get a bonus scene from the first novel, *Nemesis*, showcasing a ménage à trois between Scarlet, Lillith, and Fallon. You'll also get a link to a free novella that explores the story of Watcher and Scarlet, called *Origin.*

You can also grab the novella in the bundled set of the first phase of Heroes and Villains, also available in paperback.

WHAT'S next in the Heroes and Villains World?

Persephone is gearing up for the final show down to face Niberu and save Earth. But her only chance for a future lies in a past she's unwilling to face.

The Heroes and Villains saga comes to its explosive finale with the sixth book in this scorching hot organized crime romance series that brings your superhero fantasies to life...

PERSEPHONE: The Villain Queen

The Hive: Her worst enemy . . . and the only one who can save her

I SPENT centuries trying to both avenge my home and stop the destroyer Niberu from wreaking his chaos on other planets.

But I have failed.

And now, Niberu is on Earth.

I will need all my allies to combat him. My closest confidante and her Watcher; my winged fighter and his new wife; my ex-Hero and his two lovers; my child and her Steel Soldier; Niberu's turncoat daughter and the new CEO of Heroes Org; my brother and his scientist with her monster.

There is one other I know would bolster our ranks. One who sits in my own dungeon for crimes unatoned.

Letting him out may save this planet . . . but it would destroy my heart.

ABOUT THE AUTHORS

Liza Penn and Natasha Luxe are a pair of author friends with bestselling books under different names. They joined forces—like all the best superheroes do—for the greater good.

You can keep up with them at their newsletter. Located at http://rarebooks.substack.com, they often feature links to freebies and bonus material.

For more information about all their books and extra goodies for readers, check out their website at thepennandluxe.com.

[f]

ALSO BY LIZA PENN & NATASHA LUXE

Printed in Great Britain
by Amazon